Meandering

Stories of Past, Present and Future

by Vera Mont and Francis Mont

CONTENT

Drive Safely
by Vera Mont

It can be a pretty decent existence, driving a rich man and his family wherever they all need to be. Take him to the airport, business meetings; her, to dress fitting or DAR luncheon; the children, to oboe lessons and rugby practice. Find the place, keep the passenger comfortable, get there on time, wait outside — simple. My favourite destination is a dude ranch, where they go for family bonding some weekends.

Horses and cows haven't much conversation, but the dogs are friendly. They like cars. Anyway, those have always been easier trips than city driving. There is so much to be aware of in the city, so many obstacles and dangers to watch for. Still, I always did good work. The boss was satisfied and I was happy enough.

Now everything's changed. The job's become so stressful, I don't know how I can keep on doing it.

For instance, look there: a stout woman walking a dog. The dog is on leash; odds are 25 to 1 against it running out into the road. The woman is even less likely to, and I estimate her top speed no more than 3 kph, in a sprint. Not too hard to calculate her trajectory and avoid a collision. No problem with the ethics, either: if I can't avoid both, hit the dog. Those are my orders; I don't get a choice. Okay so far.

Now, look over there. Three males in their early twenties, bumping and shoving one another as they walk along, laughing and honking as they do when inebriated, not paying attention. They may suddenly change course and lurch into the crosswalk up ahead, or even jaywalk anywhere. I have to watch out for that possibility.

I must try to anticipate a new direction and estimate their velocity. I have to calculate the variables for each possible scenario: if they split up, one or two change course and one or two either continue on or stop. See what I mean? If I were unprepared and couldn't stop in time to avoid running them over, I'd have to decide which way to turn. On the left is oncoming traffic.

Moving at or below the speed limit, a head-on collision would not kill my passenger, though it would surely injure him. I can't tell who's in the other vehicles, whether they're wearing seat belts, whether they're alert enough to brake or veer off, whether they have infants on board, or what. So I'd opt for the sidewalk. It's clear just now, because who wants to be anywhere near those louts?

There's a comfortable 15-meter gap between lampposts, but they're actually safer to hit at this speed than a cement wall; my passenger would suffer airbag bruises and seatbelt abrasions; at worst, a fractured clavicle or nose. Hitting a parking meter is preferable; one of those can stop a car, all right, and leave a big dent in the hood. Pricey bodywork, but the insurance company will spring for it. Not a lamppost collision, though; they'll write off a vehicle for that.

A mailbox is a safer alternate target, but those things will go flying. There's a 47% probability of a pedestrian coming from the opposite direction, and a 14% chance of causing that person serious injury. Fatality is down around 1% or 1.5%. Even so, try not to hit mailboxes.

Now, if there are more pedestrians on the sidewalk, the risk depends on how many, how far apart and their speed of approach. It might not be possible to avoid all of them and still keep my passenger safe. If I have to choose between an executive carrying a briefcase and a matron carrying a baby, the woman has a higher priority rating; I would hit the man. A couple with a child, that's three people, just like the three young men, only more valuable, so I'd spare them and hit the drunks instead.

Three old people, on the other hand, are worth less than three young people, even if they're sober, unless one or more has a socially significant occupation. How can you tell a neurosurgeon from a loan shark? A pregnant woman takes precedence over a flat woman of the same age, but not a child under 12... Or is it a child under 6?

Oh, crap, I'll never get the hang of my new ethical subroutines!

First Contact

by Francis Mont

We have only one TV set in the lounge of the hospital's closed ward and, usually, we bicker about what to watch. The last few weeks, however, we had no arguments; everyone was glued to CNN, watching the alien spaceship over one city or another.

It appeared one day, hovered over New York, hung motionless in the air for a week. Nobody saw or heard it coming; it just appeared suddenly and obscured quite a lot of the sky. It resembled nothing science fiction writers had ever invented. It had a rectangular shape, like a floating breadbox, not something built for speed. It did not land, did not respond to hundreds of attempts at communication by private and military agencies. Then, one day, it simply disappeared from the New York sky, only to appear at the same moment over Rio de Janeiro, then Cairo, Moscow, Berlin, Tokyo. At each place, it spent a few days and then moved on.

It seemed to enjoy the spectacle of a bull fight, hovering over Spain, it visited all the famous walls on the planet: the Great Wall of China; the wall between the *Gaza* Strip and Israel; the new wall under construction between the US and Mexico; the remnants of the Berlin wall.

It appeared fascinated with the Tokyo night, with the city ablaze with light. Then we watched it as it made a visit to the oil extraction sites in the northern Alberta tar sands, then hopped over to the calving Childs Glacier in Alaska where some thrill-seekers were surfing the huge waves created by the melting and collapsing ice blocks.

We laughed our heads off, watching it over Vatican City, where the terrified Easter Sunday pilgrims threw themselves on the ground in a frenzy of prayer. It was a different scene over Jerusalem, where pilgrims at the Wailing Wall greeted it as the long awaited Messiah.

I have always heard voices in my head, random thoughts from people around me, but there was nothing menacing in the glimpses I experienced of these alien minds, nothing suggesting evil intentions. My fellow inmates guessed wildly about the purpose of the visit. Some thought it was a survey mission for possible invasion, others were convinced that it meant to unite humanity by drawing fire against a potential common enemy.

That idea gained some credence when we observed the spaceship hovering over Kashmir, above the raging war between India and Pakistan. It did not interfere with the barrage of missile and artillery fire the two armies were raining down on each other's heads. Some frightened idiots from both armies tried to shoot it down, but the missiles simply disappeared halfway along their trajectory. The aliens did not retaliate or respond; they stayed a few more hours and then resumed hopping from continent to continent, metropolis to metropolis.

They never revealed themselves, nobody discovered what they looked like; nobody had any idea what they wanted. And then, one day it was gone without a trace, without any attempt to communicate.

This last statement is not entirely true.

I heard their farewell telepathic message, apologizing for the intrusion and thanking us for our matchless entertainment value. They said they would be back to get more video footage for The Galactic Comedy Show, which specializes in irrational species and their hilarious behaviour.

Leap Year

a short story in four parts

by Vera Mont

1.

Four long years he'd waited in suspense.
His leap-year theory might prove wrong. The
ancient building that housed this modest watering
hole might have been demolished or converted.
Rodgers had become a regular at The Wagon and
Horses, visiting the gents' regularly. He always
found it, too, there in the basement.

Only last February 29th had been different. In the
dim light, he'd missed his step at the half-landing,
groped for the suddenly absent hand-rail,
stumbled and lurched sideways. Instead of a
painful impact, however, the wall had ... What?
dissolved? dematerialized?... and he'd stepped
into a traditional inn-yard, right out of some BBC
costume drama. Where the asphalted car park
had been for half a century, now were
cobblestones underfoot, and outbuildings from
another age.

It had given him quite a turn, that first time. But,
beer pressing more urgently than fear, he had
sought relief against the stable wall. Returning by

the same route, had found the pub unchanged and himself none the worse. Braced with a brace of whiskies, he'd gone back exploring through the - door? - that wasn't there.

He'd walked around the main building to the front entrance, where he'd stood for a long moment and gazed up at the shingle depicting a gormless great farm conveyance and two hefty Clydes in bad perspective. Inside, the furnishings looked somewhat newer; the bartender, a little older and much wider; the all-male clientele, quaintly attired. That was when he'd noticed the wall calendar over the bar. Sunday February 29, 1808. That, too, was when he'd overheard one of the guests address his companion: "I say, Constable, how did the sketching go today? You must be chilled to the bone." Yes, by Gum, the famous John Constable, supping on brown ale and kidney pie like any mortal man.

Rodgers had stumbled through a door in time, no less! Never one to snub Opportunity when she knocked, he ordered a pint, downed it quickly, then abstracted the pewter stein in which it was served, plus a fur-lined hat from the coat-rack, as he sidled out the front door. He nipped along the forecourt and through the temporal portal. The stolen items came through perfectly. He was once more in the same pub, in 1988.

Aha! He'd wait awhile, 'till the painters got well into their cups and the landlord was fully occupied, before returning to the past. Unnoticed, he would pussyfoot up to Constable's room, slip out with a masterpiece or two, then back to 1988. A sound plan. Only, just as he'd embarked on that crucial last trip to the gents', the bartender had announced closing. Midnight - and his private door into the past had also closed.

Here he was again, on February 29, 1992. And here was the portal, as he'd hoped. He went through it, to find the same courtyard; same damp wind redolent of horses, piss and stale beer. He rounded the building, entered through the front door in 1808, noted the same group of young men by the hearth, the burly innkeeper.... who saw him, too, and moved unwonted nimbly.

Laying ham-fists to Rodgers' lapels, he growled: "You han't paid for your drink. And where's me mug?"

One of the customers chimed in: "My good winter hat's missing, as well."

Rodgers, no stranger to tight corners, knew he'd talk himself out of this one, given a little time. They could prove nothing: they found no stolen property on his person.

A painter said, "He's probably hid them in the stable. Hold him fast while we search." And they all trooped off excitedly.

Locked in the dark pantry, an eternity later, he heard them returning empty-handed. At last he'd be set free! Then, clearly above the disappointed hubbub, he heard the landlord: "Time, gentlemen! Time!" But, but… it was too early! His luminous watch dial read just on 11…Oh. Sunday. Bloody Sunday!

2.

Four long years he'd waited. Trapped by early closing and the matter of some missing articles - who'd've thought a hat could cost so much!? - in 1808, in a godforsaken Essex country inn. Well, a late 20th century man of Rodgers' resourcefulness didn't waste too much time mucking out stables. A good deal on his novelty time-piece here, a spot of pilferage there, a more fashionable coat; a friendly wager hither, a better class of pigeon; a shrewd investment yonder… Having studied the Napoleonic wars in upper third finally paid off. He had travelled a bit, adapted and prospered.

He owned a dozen Constables - honestly, if inexpensively, purchased. No great unwieldy six-footers, of course; neat, portable little studies, unframed. They'd fetch a tidy fortune in his own time. And not sold through some gouging fence, either! With bona-fide provenance, he could approach Christie's of London if he liked. With one picture at a time, of course; no sense flooding the market.

If the portal would open.... *If* it would lead to 1992.... Rodgers checked his gold fob-watch yet again. Almost noon: opening time. For this momentous occasion, February 29, 1812, he had returned to the Wagon and Horses by carriage, as a respectable patron. The landlord's effusive greeting made a nice change from his previous reception.

The courtyard hadn't changed. There was the service door, as it should be. Holding his precious carpet-bag even more closely than his breath, Rodgers took a cautious peek inside. Just as it should be. Dim half-landing, no hand-rail, shabby staircase. He stepped through the portal.

Up the half flight of stairs, past the pay-phone in its murky alcove, a pair of swing-doors had been installed. He went on through to the tap-room, and strolled among the patrons. He peered casually over a man's shoulder at his newspaper. February

29, 1996. Close enough. Rodgers exhaled a jubilant sigh and surveyed his modern local of fond recollection. More women about than he remembered, lunching, exhibiting vast tracts of skin and some unladylike vocabulary. More greenery than he was used to, both on the plates and in hanging baskets. Still, pretty much in order.

Taking the minimum time needed for reconnaissance and none at all in a vain effort to recover assets long since claimed by his creditors, nor visiting his erstwhile digs, nor attempting to change his antique suit (rather more elegant than its contemporary variant, anyway,) Rodgers went directly to City Center and chose the poshest of three art galleries for an appraisal.

"They're good," said the dealer. "Excellent. Confident brush-work, fine gradation of colour. Who painted them?"

What kind of ignoramus, Rodgers thought, passes for an art expert nowadays? "Why man, can't you recognize an early Constable? Preliminary studies - never exhibited, never catalogued."

"Just what I'd have said, at first glance. The forger is *very* good indeed. Tell him next time to take at least a stab at aging his work. Why, one can literally *smell* the fresh paint!"

3.

Rodgers was not about to wait another four years. It was barely 2p.m. on February 29th, 1996. His private door in time stayed open for another ten hours. If he could not sell authentic Constables in his own era.... Well then! He would take modern merchandise into the past, when a pound was actual sterling.

What merchandise? Something small. Not electrical, obviously. Art was too fickle; gold, too risky. Analyze the market to which he had access. Oh, he could find plenty of men in the nineteenth century, with more money than sense. But there wasn't time. Having been trapped in the past for four years, Rodgers was not keen to wait out another cycle.

The answer, when it struck him, was so obvious, he laughed aloud. All the guests at the inn had been artists. Why, they'd stand on line to buy paint that looked for all the world like oil, but cleaned up with water and dried overnight! He could unload a satchelful in under an hour. He need only nip out through the gents' in 1996, stroll in the front door in 1812, sell his wares, and be back with the lolly, well before closing.

The most brilliant side-effect of this plan would be

confounding the art-experts. What would the pompous bastards say when genuine Constables, Millaises and Turners started popping up, done in modern acrylics? Ah, sweet revenge!

Rodgers worked fast. He hit the biggest art-supply store in Chelmsford, and re-entered The Wagon nonchalantly, if somewhat short of breath, before the singles crowd became too thick. He stopped at the bar for a quick bracer, then headed for the lavs. Light on the half-landing was still dim. Good. Handrail ends; wall; push. Smell of damp wind, ale and stable-yard, all copasetic.

"Pardon me..."
What? Someone behind him!
"I was looking for the powder room..."
Rodgers wheeled about, laid hands on the damned interfering bird, his only intent to shove her back into the late 20th century. But she somehow got the wrong idea. Uncanny strong, too. Knocked him ass over teakettle onto the muddy stones and ran along the courtyard, yelling her silly head off. He had to stop her! Heading for light, the terrified girl stumbled through the front door of the inn, with Rodgers in limping pursuit. Half a dozen strong men seized hold of him before he could formulate a single coherent thought.

Oh, bollocks!

4.

How would Rodgers muck it up *this* time? The past four years had been eventful enough for one life. What with having had to explain away a scantily-clad – by contemporary standards – and panicked girl.... And then the damn fool landscape artists turning up their noses at acrylic paint... Well, even so, Rodgers had managed to eke out a not too disagreeable existence.

Lola turned out to be not a bad sort, once they'd got past the initial misunderstanding. Anyway, being trapped in the wrong century had made them natural allies. They naturally progressed to co-conspirators and finally, full partners in … let's say, skirting the law. Among other things.

Now, they could finally go home. The portal opened only on February 29th. Here, it was 1816; on the other side, 1996 - or thenabouts; the time-door was tricky.

They had returned to the Wagon and Horses a prudent two days early. They slept in the best room – cramped and basic by any century's standard, even if it overlooked the high-road rather than the barn. Food was all right, though... and the thick, dark ale! Rodgers would miss that. Also, come to think of it, he would miss horses. Perhaps the company of painters. Certainly everyone's relaxed attitude to gambling, and to a man of his age having a girl of Lolly's in tow.

He had stashed their belongings ready behind the stable - one hold-all each, to avoid notice. The arguments they'd had! A woman wants to take *everything*. Candidly, it hadn't been easy for Rodgers, either, deciding what to pack. Silver, of course: his winnings and gleanings. One fine beaver hat. A few elegant drawings by old Will Blake, more for sentiment than with any real hope of 'aging' them to satisfy modern appraisers.

After supper, he casually suggested a stroll and she agreed. Once outside, they moved efficiently, as rehearsed. Around the building, into the stable-yard, where they shed the anachronistic outer garments that covered their carefully preserved outfits from 1996. Found the service door. Interior dim, as expected; no handrail - check. Rodgers stood a moment on the half-landing to catch his breath, while Lolly charged on ahead and swung open the doors....

... on their long-time favourite waterhole, on the evening of February 29, 2000 AD. She stopped on the threshold, gazing in at a heaving mass of young bodies, half-naked and wholly mindless with alcohol and other substances. Felt through her bones, for her ears were too overwhelmed to be of any use, the beat of their primitive music.

She hesitated. "Rodgers?"
"Yes, love," he answered, hefting their bags, "just coming."
"No!" Lolly turned, scampered back down the stairs and clutched at his arm. "Please. I don't want to go in there. I just can't!"

Well, what's a besotted bloke to do? Rodgers sighed. "D'you remember where you left your cloak and bonnet?"

He supposed there would always be another leap year.

My Guardian Angel
by Francis Mont

She guides me with infinite patience to where I need to be, making sure I don't lose my way, don't make costly detours. She helps me to avoid roadblocks, traps, painful mistakes, and she insists that I always observe the Law. I can hear her voice, even when the music is blasting at full force, I hear her telling me which way to turn and how much farther I still have to go.

I don't always cooperate. Sometimes I rebel against the saintly assistance; often I am contrary and ignore the good advice, and follow my whim, just because I can. I have free will and she knows it, maybe that's why she is so tolerant: she looks upon me as a child to be humoured. She lets me throw my little tantrums, because sooner or later, she knows I will return to the correct path. Then she resumes her indulgent guidance and that makes me feel guilty, so I behave for a while.

I call her Greta, because she is so much like my dear grandmother, who never got angry with me. She knew I was a good boy, not quite grown up yet, but getting there. Now she is long gone and this voice from the sky holds her place in my life.

Once she really saved me from a very costly mistake. I had a job interview at 9:30 in the morning, at the other end of town, and I was already late setting out. I was stopped by rush hour jams every few blocks and, looking at the dashboard clock, realized I was running out of time. As I grew more and more discouraged, I was ready to give up and decided to go home. Greta told me that turning back would be a huge mistake; it would not get me where I needed to be that day. I listened to her and now I have a better job than I had been able to get in many years.

I thanked her then, but my gratitude didn't last. Just the other day, I was infuriated. I had made a mistake and wanted to correct it, quickly, impatiently, recklessly. Greta told me to slow down, take my time, make sure that I don't take sudden turns that might cause an accident.

I yelled at her then: "Do you mean to tell me that I have to drive another 2 km in the wrong direction, then turn right and, after another 1.5 km turn right again and finally come back to almost where I am now? A simple U-turn at the next driveway fixes everything!"

She stayed quiet and let me do what I wanted. Afterward, when I was back on the same road that I had exited at the wrong intersection, she resumed her calm guiding, without blame or anger, just as before.

You have to admire these GPS ladies.

Ten to the minus 43-rd of a second
by Vera Mont

Before a time classified as a Planck time, 10^{-43} seconds, all of the four <u>fundamental forces</u> are presumed to have been unified into one force. All matter, energy, space and time are presumed to have exploded outward from the original singularity.

Nothing is known of this period.

I...

... feel.

Mass, pressure. Matter. I contain and encompass matter as it also consists of and confines me.

Awareness. Thought. Words.

I am. I exist.

Outside Self is void. I have sight and yet I do not see. There is nothing to see. There is nothing. Darkness. Infinity.

I am the only Mind.

Has it always been so?

No. I remember. Before eternity, I was and yet not I: different, less. Alone, as now, but not bereft as now, for I did not then contemplate eternal solitude. Because I expected... Did I expect, or merely intuit? Hope? Yes; I anticipated Another. I remember waiting, countless eons of waiting. And then, and finally, the Other came.

Whence? From nothingness?

Infinity was different, too: not empty. There was chaos, not void; light, as well as darkness. Dimension, distance. It was good, I think. It was out of reality the Other came to meet me.

We knew. Not immediately, at first glance: we began in mutual ignorance which nonetheless contained a sweet familiarity. We gave and received thought, recognition. And recognizing, loved, and loving, embraced. That embrace included everything: I, the Other, the universe merged - into the One which is the present I.

And there was sleep and waking: a Cycle.

Loneliness.

I wake to sorrow. Loss. It is not good.

I desire an end to loneliness. I wish that consummation once again, even if oblivion must follow.

Do I have choice? Can I alter what is?

If I have the attribute of preference, surely choice, too, is in my constitution. That which I am capable of wanting, I must be also capable of attaining. Matter can be felt: does it follow that matter can be affected?

To whom do I speak? No answer. Am I addressing only myself? Or Thee, my unknown friend – twin, mate, companion, completion - for whom I so yearn; who must come to me in the fullness of time.

There is no time, only eternity. Yet I remember what has been and question what may be. I have language for time: now, always, before, hereafter. That which is possible to name is possible.

In time, there can be motion. Motion is change.

I can conceive of time. I must therefore be able to engender motion. I contain all that is capable of movement. If I move, everything changes. If I stretch, matter must expand. If I shrug, this dense and heavy mass will shift, fall away and free me of its burden.

Freedom from, I understand. But free to... do what?

Matter is the fabric of my being. In disrupting it, should I also derange myself? Must pain be added to bereavement?

Can I bear it?

If matter dissipates in randomness, will Mind also dissolve in chaos? Are my thoughts a function of my substance or something apart, transcendent? Would identity, spirit, continue beyond extrication from mass?

I have slept and awakened. After the consummation and the sleep, I am in possession of my faculties: awareness, thought, sensation, potency, dread. Is it then possible for me to cease?

I am all, yet I do not know all.

I cannot know my limits, but by testing them.

Death.

This is a concept more abstruse than time, more fearful than pain, fully as awesome as eternity. I do not want to die. Am I sufficiently unhappy to attempt a change and risk annihilation?

Life is order. If I am to survive... if my mind is to remain intact through a rearrangement of matter, that rearrangement must follow a plan. If mind is, as I have postulated, truly distinct from matter and has pre-eminence, then...

Will.

If I am able to impose my will upon matter, then...

I can order chaos, separate light from darkness, lift being out of nothingness. I can organize matter; divide it into parts, portions, particles: I can build with it, mold it, fashion it according to my need. With the power of my Word, I can...

Create.

Out of matter I can call forth Life, mind, sentience - an entity: a companion. Would that be good? Is that my desire?

Yes!

I shall form a likeness of Myself, endow it with the breath of life, and thus create a... Man. But first, I should prepare him room. Yes, I shall put a great disc into space, a firm rock for the man to stand upon, overarched by a pellucid firmament, in which to hang a dazzling golden fire by day and dimmed lanterns at night. According to these lights shall the man reckon time.

 I will smooth the ground at his feet and cover it with soft vegetation; make the breeze that touches his skin fragrant and warm - for this creature will be fine and fragile, in need of tender care. I will make beasts to browse upon the land and flying creatures to populate the air: birds, fowls, butterflies. I will divide the water from the land, and to enliven the waters, create fishes, serpents, tortoises.

I will design a wondrous diversity of animals that run and climb, swim and slither, glide and flutter. And all these things, yes, even the grasses and the trees, shall be fruitful and multiply. When I have set the man in the midst of this garden, I will make another of his kind, for it is not good to be alone, as I am. I will give the man and his mate dominion over the beasts and the fowls and fishes; let them name all creatures that dwell upon the earth. For sustenance, they shall have figs and honey, corn, yams and almonds; all that is good to eat. I will create them with eyes to see the beauty and senses to delight in my bounty. Then I will teach him my bidding, that he should please me. I shall love my creature - and the woman, also, though perhaps not so much. They will never know hunger, fear, pain or grief. They shall be happy always, and good.

Is it enough?

No. To be a fit companion for me, the man must have a mind separate from my Mind and a will independent of my Will. I shall give him an attribute akin to my own: the power to distinguish good from not good. Evil. Yes, I shall put a forbidden thing in the garden: one tree, the fruit of which man must not taste.

I will provide an advocate of evil who will counsel them to disregard my edict. Then let the man and woman determine their own fate. If they disobey and choose wrongly, I shall banish them. They will know hardship: with the sweat of his brow will the man wrest food from the earth; in pain will the woman bring forth progeny. And having ensured the continuance of their kind, they will die.

But... if I love them, to witness their suffering and death must surely hurt me also. I should prefer to save them, even if they do incur my wrath. I should open to them a means of appeasement: some offering through which they and I may be reconciled. Disobedience, resulting in want, anguish, loss of life, generation after generation - with yet a distant hope of resurrection. The sojourn of mankind upon the earth thus would be endless drama, endlessly absorbing.

For them. And for me? A question: will man succumb to the temptation I put in his path? If I wish it, how can he resist? And, having fallen, will he at last make restitution? If I supply the sacrifice and put the knife ready to hand, how can he fail? There is, after all, no real uncertainty. Pathetic manikin! Such a being can never fill but a minute crevice of my vast loneliness.

Then I shall produce, not one creature, but many. Thousands, millions, billions! Constellations of angels in samite robes, with shining faces, who will sing in clarion voices, always to glorify and to abide with me. Will that please me? For a while, I think. Measured against eternity, a very little while.

All too soon, meek adoration would grow tedious. It would require passion, conflict, suspense to hold my attention. When the hymning palls, I can divide the angels into factions, sow acrimony, pit legion against legion, each with its named supreme commander: a Prince of Darkness, a Sun-king; a nurturing Mother, a Father of Lies; a defender of harmony, a champion of discord.

I can make Titans, daemons, incubi; spirits corporeal and spirits of aether. Deities who might, in their turn, create lesser beings. Tiny amusing sprites, ponderous juggernauts; chimerae and dragons; nightmares, monsters and faeries; life-forms composed entirely of stars, entities of trailing shifting, gas.... I can populate reality with so much life that I shall never want for spectacle.

And yet...

Is it diversion that I seek? Or love?

Intimate with their every particle, originating all that drives them to action, could I ever find creatures truly engaging? They would be capable of fear, of awe, of worship... but could they ever love me as I love? Would I be less alone, though I fill a thousand thousand universes with beings so paltry? Though I create uncounted multitudes, I would yet continue solitary.

I desire, I want, I need, not imitations of my Self, feeble reflections, playthings; not to manipulate fragments of cast-off matter, but to encounter Someone.

How?

Return to the beginning.

Matter must, by its nature, my nature, contain: order and chaos, darkness and light, good and evil, being and nothingness. If I disburden matter, it will move. Motion is change. The change brought about by such an upheaval might proceed in ways I have not willed; might produce results that I cannot predict. If I set Everything in motion all at once, it may shatter, atomize, divide and separate, collide and coalesce, repel and attract, resolve itself into the elements earth, air, water, fire - and more that I have not yet begun to name. Left to itself, what might matter achieve? Universes, dimensions, bodies and spaces, world, worlds.... So many kinds of life may arise, unplanned, uncontrolled: flourish and perish; struggle, thrive and mature; live out their span and leave behind descendants like and unlike themselves.

Somewhere, somewhen, a yet unguessed, unthought-of entity may form, know itself, crawl, stand and look up; understand and feel lonely, and yearn - at last - for me, as I yearn for another. The one who comes from Self but is non-Self, different: the Other.

My companion, my completion.

Imagine!

No. No. I imagine too much. I have imprinted words, forms, sentiments upon a portion of my fabric: predestined it to play out these conjectures. It cannot be destroyed. In wishing for mere entertainment, have I already doomed my cherished purpose? Is all the future tainted by this unworthy dream? Perhaps not: it was but a brief notion; little substance is compromised. Shall I set it apart, to keep the rest pure? Or shall I refrain from this last intervention?

I must think no more, lest my words influence all that begins, all that may evolve. I must not will, but only wait and hope.

Have I decided, then?

Yes. I shall, I must, attempt, not a created, ordered universe, but an unknowable event. I shall, I must, risk agony, diffraction, even the loss Consciousness. I shall, I must, chance everything, for Chance is the only means to ultimate fulfillment.

Then:

Let it be.

The Trap

by Francis Mont

Jeff Grey was mad as hell. Relations with his manager kept going from bad to worse. Everyone knew he was the most brilliant software designer in the department but, instead of reward and recognition, the boss gave him more of this crap about "insufficient experience" and "not ready to handle supervisory responsibilities".

The last straw was Susan. He might forgive everything else, but the way Barry used his position to lure her away from Jeff was too much. Jeff had spent months making her term here a co-op student's dream-come-true. Then, just when he was working up the nerve to ask her out, Barry had to come along and bawled him out – for tardiness, of all the bullshit pretexts…he felt humiliated and betrayed..

Jeff spent a long time staring at the wall, thinking about what he should do to teach Barry a lesson.

~

Barry Winter was puzzled. He couldn't figure out Susan. She was a smart kid, attractive in a trendy, but unsophisticated way and showed promise - well worth considering as a recruit. This was her last year at City College and Barry had been planning to offer her a job at term's end.

But lately, she'd started acting oddly. A vain old fool might even think she was coming on to him. That made no sense. With interns, male or female, he was careful always to maintain a strictly business attitude. So, why was Susan going out of her way to remark on dumb things like his necktie, or coo over his importance in the firm? What on Earth was she up to?

She got along well with everybody, even Jeff, which was really surprising. Jeff regularly made co-op students' life hell, he could not forgive anybody not knowing as much as he did. He was so intolerant of beginners, you would think he had been born knowing everything.

There was no doubt, Jeff was the department's genius; in spite of himself, Barry got to rely on Jeff's ability to overcome serious obstacles. Time was always short, the all-powerful 'accountants' were constantly breathing down his neck, he found himself taking short-cuts far more often than he liked to admit.

And Jeff had such an unusual mind, looking at each problem as if he had never seen anything like that before, coming up with solutions where no solution was possible. But Jeff was a loose cannon and Barry was constantly worried about him.

There was a suppressed anger in the boy, an anger that wanted to put people down, to punish them for some unnamed crime they were all guilty of. Lately he noticed some really troubling mood swings with the kid, as if he really wanted to lash out at someone.

"Find the cause", he told himself time and time again; "find the cause, you will have found the solution".

~

Susan Blair arrived early at the "New Horizon" sub-orbital rocket company. She liked to get up early, face the day with a still empty office, where she could relax and get ready for the day gradually, as her colleagues arrived.

Having this quiet time, she was free to let her mind wander to memories of days past and expectations for the days coming. Her mind immediately focused on Jeff.

Jeff was very good looking, and boy, was he ever smart. She was always attracted by intelligence, and Jeff's IQ must be in the hundreds. Yesterday's memories bubbled to the surface: the hurt look on Jeff's face, when she responded to his timid attempt to ask her out. She didn't say no, but told him she had to think about it. She had to. Office romance was out of the question – she had learned her lesson the hard way.

She knew that she would not risk an opportunity to work here, just to find out more about Jeff; however, she was not going to give up her chance at a probably very promising relationship with him if there was no conflict with her career.

Jeff immediately took her hesitation as a rejection. Being a shy geek kind of boy, probably he did not have a lot of experience with girls, it must have cost him a lot of courage to ask her at all.

Suddenly she had a crazy idea: what if she quickly went into Barry's office and looked at his manpower-planning file? This was her last month. If they were going to make her an offer, it would show up in that file. If she was on the short list, the sooner she distanced herself from Jeff, the easier their working relationship would be. But if not… well!

She did know Barry's password, and it would only take a minute. She looked at the clock: it's only 7:21 – no way Barry, or anyone else, would get in this early.

One last look at the empty office and she walked into Barry's office, closing the door behind her. She took a deep breath, sat up straight and with one finger, carefully keyed in the eight characters of Barry's password..

~

Barry was whistling a catchy little tune to himself as he got off the elevator and sauntered towards his office. He pulled up short at the door. Something was wrong. His door shouldn't be closed. Then, through the glass, he saw Susan at his desk, staring at the screen of his PC, not typing or moving – frozen, it seemed, not even breathing.

He hesitated a few moments, taking in the scene. The girl's expression, seen from the profile, was stark, unmistakable fear. Her face was white, her eyes wide and glued to the screen; hands hovering over the keyboard, trembling slightly.

He opened the door softly and stepped into his office, expecting her to jump up in a fluster, babbling explanations or excuses or at the very least, apologies. None of that happened. Susan remained still, though she heard him enter. When she turned, he could see the sheen of sweat on her forehead.

When she spoke, her words came out as a hoarse whisper he could barely understand. "Barry, don't come any closer!"

Stopped in his tracks by Susan's tone, he said "What's going on, Susan? What's the matter with you?"

Her eyes flicked to the screen, then returned to fix on his. At last she managed coherent speech.

"Barry, whatever you do, please don't make me move from this chair. I'll explain everything, but first you have to promise to stay where you are and do nothing until you understand."

Susan's voice was little more than a whisper but carried such urgency that Barry dared not risk another step. Whatever it was, he had to wait.

"Barry, I'll show you something, only promise not to do anything, okay?"

"OK, Susan, I promise" He resolved to keep still.

"Look under your desk, Barry."

The blinds closed, only the reading lamp lit, underneath the desk was deep in shadow. The two faint glints he could discern reflected off a camera lens, and the barrel of a gun, pointed at Susan's body.

The body, he suddenly noticed, contoured on the monitor screen, with concentric circles drawn over it, centered at the midsection, exactly where the gun under the desk was pointing. And, he realized in horror, the body was moving slightly under the circles, left and right, as Susan's body swayed with the exhaustion of sitting motionless for God only knew how long.

~

Jeff Grey was bleary-eyed this morning as he walked toward his cubicle. The little sleep he had managed had been crowded with nightmares featuring police, arrest, trial and prison. He had reviewed the setup again, during the drive to work. He had gone over and over it last night, till he was sick of thinking. The plan was foolproof; no way could it fail.

His program was a masterpiece of AI - had to be, to serve the purpose. If Barry were to make a proper confession, the computer had to do better than pose "True" or "False" questions. Otherwise Barry would claim afterwards that he'd assent to anything at gunpoint.

The program must be able to determine whether Barry was telling the truth. Jeff knew some facts about last year's security scandal. He knew that Barry was involved and that he'd deleted files from the server and the backup database. Forcing Barry to confess publicly would kill two birds with one stone: Barry would be fired and Susan would see him for the crook he really was. Maybe she'd finally see who the hero was, too.

They could not prove he was behind the scheme. They probably would know; after all, who had enough brain here to dream up this fantastic scheme, never mind implementing it. But there was no proof: the program would erase from memory on termination or, even on power-loss; it was not stored on disk or tape, there were no printouts.

He reviewed the critical phase again:

- Barry sits down at his keyboard, powers on.

- Jeff's program, starting automatically, prompts Barry for password as usual.

- If password incorrect, terminate program.

- If password is Barry's, instruct him not to move from chair and to look under the desk. – Barry sees gun and camera, aimed at his flabby gut.

- Explain the setup, convince Barry there is no escape. The gun will fire if he tries to leave the chair, interfere with the gun, the camera or the computer.

- Live feed interrogation to the department's public Mailbox.

- Caution Barry that the gun will go off if the program identifies a false statement. Barry does not know what facts the program 'knows', so he will not dare to tell any lies. He can't count on bluffing, pleading or bluster; he can't look for mercy or sympathy or reluctance from a machine.

- At top of screen, display the image of Barry's torso as captured by the camera, superimposed with concentric circles, indicating how far his body can move without triggering the gun. This serves both as warning and psychological pressure.

- Give audio and visual alarms if body's captured and locked image starts approaching trigger-zone.

He had given up finding faults in his logic, it was foolproof, it could not fail: he would have his revenge. With this thought, he sank onto his own chair. He had resolved to act naturally, resisted the temptation even to look toward Barry's office.

~

It took Susan a few minutes to explain what had happened. Admitting her little scheme now seemed trivial, just a lead-in to the crucial matter, convincing Barry that the trap was inescapable. She had spent the last hour thinking about ways to defeat it and found none.

The program had prepared her for the shock of the gun pointing at her body, enough to help control her muscles tensing to hurl her out of the chair, out of harm's way. She knew that there was no escape; in a crazy way, the image of her body moving slightly beneath those circles was more convincing than the cold logic displayed on the screen.

She could see right away that she'd blundered into a trap set for Barry. Evidently, it meant to force him to confess some old security violation she'd never heard of before. The program was presenting facts she didn't know and demanding answers she didn't have.

If the computer were to decide 'Barry' lied, she was the one who'd be shot. So she used all her creativity to stall the procedure, to give true but evasive answers, hoping that Barry would arrive soon, not daring to think what would happen if he was late or did not show up.

The program pursued her -- pressing, demanding, forcing her into logical inconsistencies and contradictions, trapping her into no-win situations. She'd begun to fancy that it 'suspected' her stalling and was growing impatient, more and more threatening.

With a set time limit for every answer, she had to keep typing evasive answers even while trying to convince Barry to take over the keyboard and admit whatever the program wanted him to admit. She did not know how much longer she'd last. She'd been going on adrenalin for almost an hour and was about ready to crash. Her body ached from the stiff posture and her temples were throbbing, her mind was wandering when she so desperately needed to concentrate.

~

Barry was recovering his faculties. Watching Susan fight for her life against that gleaming camera lens, unable to move away from the dark and deadly circle of the gun's muzzle, he had gone from shock to fear to anger in seconds. Now he was shaken by a rage such as he had never experienced.

This had to be Jeff's handiwork. Nobody else would, or could, do something this crazy. He understood that the younger man was immature, full of resentment and grievance. Mad enough to lash out …but murder? He'd never suppose Jeff for a cold-blooded killer.

What should he do? The only way to save Susan seemed to confess his 'crime'.

That confession would ruin his career. From what he could see in these few minutes, the program contained accurate information about those events of last year that still haunted Barry with regret.

If only it had worked, if only he had been able to make his superiors recommend aborting the launch, the tragedy might never have happened. He had deliberately manufactured false evidence that the on-board computers were unreliable, evidence that would have taken weeks to evaluate, gaining time for the rocket engineers to prove the fatal flaw in the engine. He had promised his best friend on the project, a rocket engineer who had pleaded for his help the night before.

He had done it in vain, he never had a chance to submit his report: the rocket exploded next morning. Afterwards, the only thing he could do was to erase every trace. It served no more purpose, and it would have gotten him fired.

Jeff must have suspected him of complicity when he had erased all the files and backup tapes from the project archive documents. That was the only possible explanation. It could not be anybody else but Jeff.

Susan kept typing in unsatisfactory replies. Periodic warnings on the screen kept coming faster, in bigger red letters – each one more dire than the last.

Between questions, she looked up at him, each brief glance filled with desperate intensity. Of course he could not let that silly girl die! He had no choice.

Unless - the thought was as sudden as unexpected - unless Jeff knew a way out. It was his program, after all (had to be!)

Barry had spent half a lifetime to get where he was, to earn the trust of his colleagues, the respect of his peers in the field. Would he let it be destroyed without a fight? He had to try, even at the risk of straining the program's patience even further.

~

"Grey, get your ass in here!"

Barry's voice was decisive and serious; the voice of authority, not the plea of a cornered criminal. Jeff felt sick to his stomach. Steady! Even if Barry discovered the trap and guessed who was responsible, there was no proof. No fingerprints, no hairs or fibers. Jeff had been meticulous. Just keep denying, no matter what, he told himself.

He was half expecting to find Barry down on the floor, inspecting the device under his desk, not standing like a statue in the middle of a dim office, with – Oh God! When he caught sight of Susan at the terminal, he very nearly lost his breakfast. Susan's frail figure, swaying with fatigue, mirrored by the image on the screen; her pale, strained face; the error message – blinking red, which was a level three warning… …she was losing. She hadn't even been here last year; her responses came from studied protocol, guess-work and office gossip. What could she know?

Jeff could not bear the sight. For a split second he felt an insane hatred for the program that was torturing his girl. But there was also vindication, and pride in the success of his creation. Emotions raced around in his mind: pride, confusion, resentment, fear, and - finally - defiance.

He was not going to admit anything.

"What's up, Barry?" he asked his boss in the cool, practical voice he had been using with him recently.

"You know damn well, what's up" Barry hissed, "I don't care why you did it, but you better stop this insanity before somebody gets hurt!"

"Stop what?"

"Jeff, there is no time to waste on nonsense, I know it and you know it, and Susan is in danger. Defuse that goddamn program!"

Barry was shouting now.

Jeff remained cool. Brazen it out, he might still win.

"What's going on?" he asked. "Looks like somebody wants answers. You better provide them, Barry, they're getting mad."

They stared at each other, eyes filled with hate and pain.

The machine now emitted a burst of short, shrill beeps, "FINAL WARNING" flashed on the screen. Susan, paralysed in her chair, unable to respond, let her hands fall into her lap, and just sat, helplessly gazing at the two men.

It was Barry who looked away first. His body visibly sagged: a broken man, accepting defeat. He quickly took over the keyboard, careful not to obstruct the camera, stared at it for a few seconds and then started typing. The beeping stopped. The red flashing message disappeared and was replaced by rapid-fire questions that ran across the screen. Barry typed without hesitation, apparently having forgotten all about Jeff and

Susan, who stared at him, mesmerized. The only sound in the room was his clicking.

Jeff's emotions were in turmoil. He ought to feel triumphant; instead, he felt like crap. He now realized Barry could have turned around and walked out, unharmed, any time. He could have feigned ignorance, called for help; could have got off scot free. The gutless, unscrupulous careerist Jeff had been seeing in him the last few months would have done just that.

Instead, here he was, sacrificing his career to save a stupid girl who got herself in this trouble by sneaking around.

Jeff glanced at the screen. Barry was typing away, forced by the program closer and closer to the point where the evidence against him would be final. For the second time that morning, Jeff felt an irrational hatred of his own brilliant work. There was something evil in its cold, ruthless pursuit: the machine beating down the human. Such an unequal contest!

"Wait!" he put a hand on Barry's shoulder, "let me try to kill it. I don't know who did this, but I think I may be able to abort the program"

Barry wiped his forehead, stepping aside from the keyboard without a word.

Jeff typed rapidly for a long time. It was the greatest challenge he ever faced. He was fighting his program, his own creation. He had made it unbeatable. He had to beat it. For a second, he chuckled crazily, remembering the college student's conundrum: "Can God make a stone too heavy for God to lift?"

The program was winning. It was clearly running out of patience. The red warning messages reappeared, flashing more menacingly than ever. The beeping started, shrilly, loudly, and the words "LAST WARNING" appeared on the screen. The image of a clock ticking off toward zero appeared over the circles strangling Susan's body, and the animated image of the gun, trigger being slowly squeezed, appeared pointing at a red coloured heart placed inside the image of the body.

Susan screamed.

Barry swept Jeff's hand aside, snatching the keyboard, typing in the answer that they both knew would seal his fate.

It happened as if in slow motion.

Jeff tried to wrest the keyboard back from his boss. He was beyond reason; could not accept defeat from anything – not anything! – even himself.

Barry pushed at him violently, hurling him at the wall, making him stumble and crumple to the floor next to the power-bar, hitting his head on the desk on the way down. It was this final blow that seemed to rouse him, as if from some fever dream. The insane glitter faded from his eyes as he stared intently at his mentor.

The virtual pointer approached zero.

Susan stopped breathing.

Barry reached for the keyboard once again, to type in the single word the program demanded: the key word for the incriminating transaction record in the undeletable log-file buried deep in the archive tapes. Without this key no proof against him existed.

The three sounds were simultaneous.

The click of the first letter of the word Barry was typing, the click of the switch on the power-bar, the click of the firing pin of the gun beneath the table-top.

Time stopped.

It seemed like an eternity before Barry and Susan realized that the gun had not fired.

They both stared at Jeff, his hand still resting on the switch.

"You bloody, murderous bastard!" Barry shouted " you almost killed her!"

Jeff looked back at him with a curious mixture of pain and happiness in his eyes. Oddly, there was no belligerence left in his expression, it was almost serenely relaxed. He looked like a man who had grown years, in a matter of seconds; like somebody who'd made a decision about questions haunting him most of his life.

"Barry, I'm sorry! I misjudged you completely. You are the most decent human being I know."

"What about Susan, you insane maniac?!" Barry shouted, still in shock over what so nearly happened.

"You don't really think I loaded the gun?" Jeff said, slowly getting to his feet - "You can call the cops now."

They stared at one another for a long time, the three of them, each looking at the other two for signs of decision.

Finally, Susan spoke, her voice shaky. "Jeff, you goddamn crazy bastard, you owe me the biggest, most expensive dinner your miserable salary can afford, for what you put me through today!"

Jeff looked questioningly at Barry, who stared back at him with a murderous scowl.

"If this program of yours weren't the most brilliant piece of software I have ever seen, I would let you rot in jail the rest of your life." He slumped down in the chair Susan hastily vacated in response to his impatient gesture.

"You both get the hell out of here. I have work to do".

The Ring

by Vera Mont

Donna-Lou Ribble used to meet Stanley Buckminster Waterhouse IV under a big old weeping willow on the riverbank below the Waterhouse estate. She would take a cunning round-about route from town; Stanley had only to stroll across his grandmother's garden and duck through the lilac hedge.

They had to be quiet since the old lady always left her bedroom window open. Still, it was a fine, private place for stealing kisses. More than kisses, too: a couple of times, they'd gone all the way. But it was all right, because they were truly in love and would get married one day soon.

When one or the other could not get away, they left a note in a hollow of the tree, just like star-crossed lovers in some romantic movie. This afternoon, Donna-Lou found one of Stan's notes. It sounded urgent: "Meet me at 8 tonite. I really need to see you."

Under the folded piece of paper, laid carefully in a bed of moss, she found a ring. It had a huge blue stone in the center, surrounded by eight smaller white ones, in a setting of gold filigree. It was a bit loose on her finger and a bit on the gaudy side…

What do boys know about jewellery? Besides, things always look better in the catalogue. She thought it beautiful anyway, because dear Stan had picked it out. Even if, after getting his inheritance, he were to replace it with a proper diamond, she would treasure this token forever.

At last! Stanley had been trying for two months to get up the nerve to tell his rich, snooty grandmother that he loved the daughter of a backhoe operator. Mr. Ribble made a decent living at the gravel pit, and that would just have to be good enough for the Waterhouses. For their own part, Donna-Lou's own family were bound to have fits when she told them she was marrying a Protestant, but they'd just have to lump it. The truth was finally out.

After dinner, she took the ring from her pocket, slipped it onto her engagement finger, took a deep breath and made her announcement. First, there was silence. Then her dad threatened and swore, until his face went purple. Her mother wept and pleaded. Her big brother called her unprintable names. There was a lot of yelling and crying, through which Donna-Lou staunchly stood her ground. Then she was sent upstairs while they argued over what to do with her.

At 7:30, she climbed out her bedroom window onto the porch roof and let herself down the ten-foot drop to the lawn. It was the second bravest thing Donna-Lou had done in that one hour - and in her whole life. At five minutes past 8:00, she limped into the shadow of the willow branches, and the waiting arms of her beloved.

"Oh, Stan," she sighed, "I'm so happy!"

"Yeah, me too, Babe," he mumbled into her hair, running eager hands down her back and over her hips. "It's been too long."

Donna-Lou broke the embrace, gently pushing him off. He must not get carried away just yet; there was too much to talk about. He looked down at her hand where the big ring flashed in a ray of setting sun.

"That's Gran's sapphire."

"You mean, it's *real*?" She had known that the Waterhouses must accept her, in time, but had never dared hope for immediate approval, let alone a blessing sealed with the matriarch's own ring. "Stan, that's wonderful! How ever did you manage? My folks will take *weeks* to get used to the idea."

Stanley didn't seem to hear. His gaze kept shifting back and forth from her face to her hand. "How did you…? How *could* you…?" he stammered. "Oh God! She's been searching all over."

Donna-Lou was not the sharpest mind in town, but it didn't take a genius to figure this out. Stan had *not* won his old relative's blessing, after all. He'd taken the ring, planning to keep their engagement secret a little while longer. She'd been too impulsive; should have talked to him before telling her parents.

"Give it here," he said. "I can probably shove it under the dresser or someplace. She'll never know."

Donna-Lou was reluctant to part with her prize. Still, this wasn't the proper way. Stan had been impulsive too. He ought to have bought her a ring himself, even a modest one; she wouldn't mind. Well, he was sorry, and it was not too late.

"All right." She shook the ring off, onto his open palm. "I don't want you to get into trouble."

"Oh, God!" he repeated. "Holy crap, yeah, she *would* think it was me…"

Donna-Lou closed his hand around the precious jewel and patted it reassuringly. "It's all right, Darling. You put this back tonight, and tomorrow, we'll go tell your granny together."

"Tell her? Tell her *what*? " Stanley stared at her with the wild eyes of a stranger. "Are you *nuts*?"

"Stan, I don't understand…"

He backed off, out of her reach. "Get away from me!"

"But, Stan…"

"Think you can blackmail me? You *must* be nuts.
A crazy thief." He took another step away, now
shaking with cold fury. "You were a nice enough
piece of ass, okay? But I can get it without all this
hassle!" He turned, casting one last hateful look
over his shoulder, then thrashed through the lilac
hedge and disappeared.

Donna-Lou slumped against the tree, dazed.
Thief? Crazy? Piece of ass? She sank down onto
the ground, not crying, not yet: tears would come
later. She was too stunned to do anything at all.

As she sat there, clutching her pain, motionless
and silent, she noticed a grey squirrel in the lilac
bush. It leapt over onto the willow tree, ran along a
branch and scurried down the trunk. From its
mouth, something long and shiny kept spilling
over, so that it had to stop every few steps to
gather up and tuck in the ends. Then it ducked
into the hollow with it treasure.

Donna-Lou remained perfectly still until the
squirrel re-emerged and scampered off among the
leafy branches. Then she cautiously reached in.
Rummaging through the moss, she lifted out the
gold chain, then came up with a necklace of pearls
and diamonds, a small pair of sewing scissors, a
fountain-pen, some coins, an ornate music-box
key and a lone ruby earring.

"Thief," she muttered. "Crazy. Blackmailer.
Floozie. Apostate. Ungrateful, wicked girl. Broke
your mother's heart. Get away from me. Ashamed
to have you under my roof." Donna-Lou sighed.
"Well….okay."

She left the scissors, the pen, the key and some
candy she found in her pocket.

Truth can hurt

by Francis Mont

John Masters, drumming his fingers on the windowpane, looked outside at the empty driveway. *She should be at home by now. The charity bazaar meeting wouldn't last this long. Was she with Conway again*?

At last, he heard the crunch of tires on the gravel, and saw Anna's red Mercedes pull up to the garage door.

"Finally!" he sighed with relief, but could not suppress his anger over the way she made him suffer.

"What took you so long?" he demanded, as she came through the door.

Anna flinched at his tone. "We had a particularly boisterous meeting, it's what took me so long." she explained in a resigned voice. "We were discussing "

"Was Conway there?" Masters interrupted.

"Michael is always there. He is the president, you know that."

"If only I could forget." John rolled his eyes. "You spend too much time with him!"

"John, I am tired. Can we have dinner now?"

John grunted. "I already ate".

"It's only seven thirty, you could have waited."
Anna sighed and walked into the kitchen to find
something to heat up.

John went back to the window.

~

"So, how was your day at the bank?" Anna asked
after she finished with the dishes.

"Wall to wall meetings, as usual" John replied,
reluctant to go into details of his business ups and
downs. Anna couldn't care less about his world.

"Let's watch some TV" he suggested.

"Good idea, there is a ballet program I have been
waiting for all week." Anna cheered up at the
prospect, but immediately deflated again. "I had
better watch it in my study".

"Would it kill you if you watched a game with me?
Just once?" He walked over to the TV set and
turned it on.

"I wouldn't enjoy it, as you well know." She looked
at him sadly and left the room.

John couldn't concentrate on the game this time.

What's wrong with us? He asked himself. *Haven't I
given her everything? She has clothes, jewellery,*

her own car, she doesn't have to work, what else could she want?

He took another sip of the scotch he was in the habit of drinking, by himself, watching television, alone.

Doesn't she know I am crazy about her, in spite of all the nutsy things she carries around in her head? All the liberal nonsense, all her charity work? I even tolerate her tree-hugging friends, for crying out loud! All I ask of her is to treat me the way I should be treated: in the social scenes I have to attend, at the parties I give, in the bedroom!

He emptied his whisky glass, letting the yellow liquid burn down his throat, spreading the sudden heat all through his body. He refilled the glass and took a smaller sip to make it last. The bottle was almost empty.

She has such a fantastic body, I think I'm addicted to it and I can never have enough. If only I knew I'm the only one with access to those gorgeous curves, I wouldn't suffer these pangs of jealousy, but how can I be sure? She attracts men and she loves the attention. And there is Conway, the jerk, and I know he wants her. Does she?

Anna was equally distracted in her study, trying to watch Swan Lake.

I can't help it, she told herself for the hundredth time. *I am really trying to be the wife he wants, but it is such hard work! Would it kill me if I watched the stupid game with him? After five years I have to admit, we have nothing in common, if we ever did! Why did I marry him?*

The ballerinas twirled and leaped across the stage, the music swelled and flowed through her mind, as she tried to find elusive answers.

Now I am paying the price with boredom every time we are together. And then, there is Mike. I admit, I am attracted to him, but it goes no further. I don't want to think about him, because, the way John spies on me all the time, not even my thoughts feel safe.

When the TV programs ended there was no way to delay the inevitable. She walked into their bedroom and started getting ready for the night. She knew what was coming, their daily routine: passionate sex on his part, passive acceptance on hers.

Will it ever change? Will I be in love again with a man I admire and who loves me for who I am? Oh Mike!

Upon her last guilty thought she was finally too exhausted to resist sleep and the dreams usually accompanying her into a less than restful oblivion.

~

John Masters put down his briefcase and buzzed for coffee - plain Columbian with cream and sugar, not one of the frothy foreign things. His in-basket was full again, though he'd cleared it last night. *Couldn't anyone down the food-chain make a decision?*

His secretary entered with a mug of steaming coffee.

"How are you, boss?" she chirped in the high, irritating voice, Masters had come to expect from young people these days.

"Thanks, Michelle, I'm fine" He tried to filter annoyance out of his voice "Fill me in on today's schedule, make sure I'm ready for the onslaught of unsolved problems" He couldn't keep his sarcasm down.

He had a hard time concentrating on Michelle's voice, his mind kept wandering back to Anna. *What is she doing this morning, and who with? She was so absent last night, was she in Conway's arms while we made love?!"* He couldn't sit still at his desk, started pacing, up and down the short stretch between his chair and the window.

John Masters was a middle aged man, with a little gray showing on his temples and a fit body. Women found him attractive and he had his share of temptation over the years. *Maybe I should respond to some of those women. Maybe it would make Anna jealous too! It would serve her right to feel what I do almost all the time! Damn, why can't I be free of her intoxicating presence, why can't I have fun like most of the guys in the club seem to?*

With a big sigh he finally sat down at his desk and focused on his job, banning the unhappy thoughts from his mind.

~

At about the same time Anna was trying to decide what to wear for the outdoor picnic organized by her group. She wanted to be both stylish and outdoorsy. Finally, she settled on a simple summer dress, long enough to let her sit on the ground with due modesty.

Mike will be there, shouldn't I wear something a bit more sexy?

She got angry at her fleeting thought.

Control yourself, stupid girl, you have never been a tease. If you don't have the courage to make a break for it, put up with your gilded cage and stop dreaming of romance!

Her family never understood why she married John. She couldn't explain it either, but suspected his newness and his difference attracted her. He seemed so strong, so confident, compared to her group of friends who were always fighting for one cause or another, despairing over the state of the world – John was like a breath of fresh air. Always optimistic, projecting hope for the future. In this age of doom and gloom she needed that hope. When John asked her to marry him, she was recently out of college, trying to decide what to do with her life. She thought with John's financial security she could have the leisure to experiment until she knew what she really wanted.

Now I know better and it may be too late. I am too used to the comfort John can provide. What would I do out there, with a Fine Art degree and no work experience? Even if I let myself fall in love with

Mike, he is not any better off. He barely makes a living as an elementary school teacher.

She shook her head as if to dislodge some troubling insects and changed her dress (too flattering to her slender figure and nicely shaped legs) to practical slacks and a loose comfortable shirt tucked into her waistband.

~

Masters was growing desperate. He could not go on like this. The doubts about Anna's fidelity were poisoning his mind with unbearable images of Anna in another man's arms. He could live with her passive acceptance, but he could not tolerate her giving her passion to another man. He had to know - he had to know for certain.

I have to find a way to know the truth. I tried spying on her and never discovered anything. I listened in on her phone calls, checked her email, followed her a few times. Either there is nothing to find or she is very discrete.

The thought he had been harbouring in the back of his mind for months now, surfaced once more. A chemistry professor he regularly played golf with at the club, kept boring his pants off with `prattle about his research into a new drug, aimed at helping and maybe curing CLD: 'compulsive lying disorder'.

The drug, according to Dr. Arthur Spencer could be administered from a spray can. It was harmless, undetectable and, once the subject inhaled it, did its biochemical trick of lowering the affected person's resistance to questions and compelled them to tell the truth.

Dr. Spencer wanted to test it, to make sure it was effective enough to justify applying for a full clinical trial. Last time they met, he'd asked Masters whether he knew anyone who might volunteer for a modest reward.

After he spent an agonizing morning still unable to focus on his work, John picked up the phone and dialled Dr. Spencer's number.

"Arthur, I found a volunteer for you" he announced.

"Oh, great" Spencer enthused, "who is he?"

"I can't tell you over the phone because he works here and I have to be discreet. Can I see you in your lab?"

"OK, bring him around before seven and we can proceed."

"See you around six thirty" John said and rang off.

~

Masters wiped his forehead before entering and forced himself to breath normally.

"So, who is your volunteer?" Arthur asked after shaking hands. "Where is he?"

"He is not here right now" John apologized, "I wanted to talk to you first to make sure that your drug really works and ready to use!"

"See for yourself," his friend said, pointing proudly to a number of small aerosol cans on his shelf – "they are loaded and ready to go. All I need is someone to try it on."

"Arthur, I need you to do me a favour. My job may depend on finding out the truth about an employee's involvement with a price fixing investigation. He is trying to blame me for it and it could get me fired. If I could make him confess "

"You don't mean what I think you mean!" Dr Spencer jumped up and stepped back in alarm. "You know fully well how illegal it would be to experiment on someone without his written consent!"

"I only want to scare the bastard by showing him the can and threaten to use it on him unless he comes clean. Could I borrow one for a day?"

"Sorry, John, I can't let you do that" Dr. Spencer's voice was final.

John knew he had only one chance and he was desperate to risk it.

Pretending to collect his briefcase, ready to leave, he brushed by Spencer's desk, knocking down a stack of papers and scattering them all over the floor. While Arthur bent down to retrieve them , he quickly reached over to the shelf and pocket one of the cans.

~

Next day, Masters took the aerosol can to work. He had a meeting scheduled with his suspect.

When asked about his involvement, the man denied and stonewalled like a pro, but when Masters, pretending to clean his monitor screen, spritzed some of the gas in the air, everything changed. Within one minute, the subject started freely admitting everything, giving the names of his accomplices, reciting dates and numbers... all without showing any awareness of his own unusual candor. Actually, he became overly friendly, recommending some homemade remedy to help Masters with his plugged up nose.

It was all the proof Masters needed. He suspended the interview and made another appointment. Let the bastard stew! Then, nonchalantly as he could bear, he left the office early. He rushed home to try the serum on his wife.

~

Anna Masters sat in her living room, staring out the window. The autumn leaves swirled around on the sidewalk, as her unhappy thoughts did in her mind.

She knew her marriage was a tragic failure. The only meaningful part of her life now was her community work. Without John's financial support, she would have to abandon the vulnerable adolescents who relied on the program she and Michael and a dozen dedicated volunteers had worked so hard to build. She knew John was blind with jealousy – he hardly bothered to conceal his spying. The interrogations to which he subjected Anna had become ever more urgent, more menacing, more humiliating. She bore them with ever less fortitude.

She was too nervous to sit idly and started cleaning the shelves in the living room. They did not need it, but the rhythmic movement of the dust cloth calmed her nerves. She needed to talk to John to resolve their unhappy situation, somehow come to an understanding and part ways in a peaceful, civilized way. When John arrived, she greeted him more warmly than usual.

During their routine "how was your day" chit-chat, John took the aerosol from his pocket and, while Anna was busy with his scotch and mixing her own drink, he let out a good long blast of the truth gas. He asked the usual questions about her activities, where she's gone, who she met, and

"So, you really like this Conway clown, do you?"

"Yes," she answered softly, "very much. And he's not a clown."

"Ever sleep with him?"

"Of course not!" she retorted hotly - more forcefully than he'd ever heard her speak. "I've never slept with anyone but you… never.. " She broke off in a sob.

Masters was so relieved, so happy, so *light*, all of a sudden! Those words were really all he'd ever wanted to hear. Anna was truly his! As he swooped her up in joyful arms, she asked, perplexed, "What is this all about?

And he told her of his jealous fantasies, the chemistry professor, the crooked VP, the truth serum, the aerosol can - the whole story, without the slightest inhibition.

As the effects of the gas began to wear off, he wondered why Anna was standing all this time, perfectly still, with a stunned expression on her face turning gradually to anger. That was the moment he realized, overcome with impatience, he had forgotten to insert his nose filters.

"Where is it?" she demanded.

Still under the influence, he produced the canister. She took it from his unresisting hand and stormed out of his house.

~

When she returned, two days later, she felt the confidence that had eluded her for most of her marriage. The last humiliation, being experimented on like a lab rat, helped her firm up the decision she had been leaning toward even before the 'trial'.

She found John sitting on the couch, staring in the air vacantly, like someone who had played his last card and lost.

"John, here is the deal" she started her prepared speech, her strong and confident voice jolting him out of his stupor.

"We will get a divorce. I will move out and take my personal things and some furniture and start looking for work. You will give me an allowance you can afford and I can live on, until I find a suitable job. I don't want to be your dependant forever. If you agree, we can part as friends."

She had arrived at the hard part of her speech, knowing it would hurt John deeply, but she had to do it.

"If not, I have the spray can as evidence and Dr. Spencer's description of how you tricked him and performed illegal experiments on me. I contacted him to find out the truth. He was outraged at your stealing his property and is willing to testify on my behalf if needs be. I don't think you can count him among your friends any more"

John knew when he didn't have a chance. He stood, looked at Anna's lovely figure, for a long moment, as if trying to etch this last image onto his brain, and silently walked out of the room.

Runaway
by Vera Mont

Everything is about death. I came to the woods because my cat died.

All her life, she'd been cooped up in a one-bedroom apartment, with no more than a quick run outside, late at night, when there wasn't much traffic, down the fire escape, through the fence and into the alley with the garbage cans. The whole time, I worried about dogs, cars and cruel boys. She always came back safely, only to die of cancer at the age of eleven. I wasted all the worry on the wrong things. I guess you never know what the right thing is to worry about until too late. If that's true, all worry is wasted - yet we can't help doing it.

There was no place, no earth, to bury her in. So I wrapped her body in the pink plaid blanket - it weighed almost nothing; just fragile bones covered in white fur – and drove north. I drove for a long time, hours and hours, and then turned off the highway onto a "No Exit" gravel road, under close trees, and another, narrower one, until it petered out in a stony, uneven track and disappeared. No fence, though of course it's somebody's land, maybe the government's. I don't really know where I am.

Nobody knows, and that's good. I came to the woods because I always said I would. Whenever things went wrong, when I made a stupid mistake, a bad decision; when Mr. Reed told me off in front of all the other tellers; after one of those confusing fights with Bruce, I used to tell myself: It doesn't matter. I'll run away and live in the woods where none of you can find me. So, when Muffin died, that's what I did. I want my tombstone to read: "She finally did."

I thought I'd got all the grief over with when the vet told me. He asked, ever so tactfully, did I want her put to sleep right away, or - ? He was kind. Is. A kind man with red hands from scrubbing. I'll never see him again. In those last weeks I took care of Muffin as best I could, learned how to give her injections for the pain, helped her to the litter box when she grew too weak, sat with her on the fire escape, I wasn't always sure about that choice. I did the right thing, though. The harder thing is usually the right one.

Muffin lies between the roots of a tall spruce, where the branches hang down low and smell good year 'round. I thumped the earth down hard and spread dry grass over top so nobody can tell where the grave is. Maybe that's the best kind of grave. On second thought, I don't want a tombstone. I miss her. I still talk to her, when I wake up from one of those nightmares where I'm running, running and something horrible keeps getting closer and I can't catch my breath, can't run fast enough. It helps to talk. When Muffin slept on my feet, I didn't need to say anything. She would lift a sleepy head and ask softly, "Crew?" Her warm, simple presence was reassuring enough.

We enjoyed that apartment, Muffin and I; it was cozy. I painted everything in soothing pastels – walls, doors, trim, second-hand furniture. I sewed curtains and slipcovers; planted a box with pink geraniums in the south window. I guess they'll die soon; Bruce won't think to water them. It was even cozier when he moved in, if a little bit cramped. I liked his masculine things in the bathroom, his clothes in the closet, his smell on the pillow. I knew we'd need a bigger place, when the time came to start a family – but the time never came.

He can stay there, as long as he keeps up with the rent. The super might ask why I'm not around. Bruce would make up a lame story about far-off relatives and Mr. Purdy will suspect that he murdered me, cut up my body in the bathtub and stashed it in dumpsters all over North York. Does Mr. Purdy have that kind of imagination? Would he act on it? Should I worry about a police search? No… That only happens in movies; normal people don't think that way. Bruce could have gotten away with murder, if he wanted to. So could I have, probably. But normal people don't.

It's okay to talk nonsense to a cat who isn't there, here. Nobody here to hear. Am I turning into a poet or just mental? Not the first time I've been called that, either. Some nights, when I'm not quite asleep, I feel a soft weight land on my sleeping bag. Twice, I thought I saw her skulking beneath a tangle of raspberry: a flash of white face, tiny white paws, silent. I wish she'd answer me, but I guess ghost cats don't talk.

That's one reason I stay. Also, it's quiet. At least, there no people noises; no baby screaming or commercial jingles, pop songs blaring from cars; no loud arguments and swearing drunks; no truck horn blasts, banging trash cans or wailing sirens. Birds and chipmunks make a surprising amount of noise, especially early in the morning. But these are happy noises. Hopeful, purposeful spring sounds. They wake me at dawn - and just as well; I can't waste kerosene staying up late. I do my scribbling by sunlight these days.

~

Today I saw a deer and fawn along the little stream. Could have watched them all day; stood perfectly still, holding my breath. Something, maybe my human smell, spooked them anyway. They didn't run off, exactly. The mother ... levitated - rose effortlessly into the air and vanished. A second later, the baby was gone too. As if they'd never been, as if I'd imagined them. Like ghosts.

Did I mean to go back? I don't recall planning to leave forever, but I must have. Why else pack all my outdoor gear and put the locker back in tidy order, so Bruce won't notice anything is missing, probably for months. What fun we had, camping, that first summer! Was it only two years ago? Bruce knew how to build a smokeless fire, catch fish, put up a tent. He was so strong and confident, so much at home in the wilderness. I was all thumbs, clueless. He showed me over and over, so patiently when I got things wrong. I learned. In the off season, I read instruction books.

Last summer, I could make and break camp, gather wood, split kindling, douse and bury the fire-pit, scale and gut fish. "Here you go," he would toss the cool silver corpses in my lap, laughing, "dinner." I could fry or boil up a pretty good meal, but I never could stomach baiting the hook or killing the fish. Bruce did that, with gusto: Whack! Whack! on a rock. Later on, when I got upset about things and threatened to run off into the woods, he used to sneer, "You'll starve to death." "I'll live on nuts and berries," I would say, "like a hermit."

There are no nuts and the tiny wild strawberries won't start appearing for another month. I did find a nice big patch of leek, some ginger vine, a precious island of fiddleheads. I keep hunting for mushrooms; morels are due any day now, and they're the best. Apple trees – fugitives from civilization, like me, tucked in among the maple and hemlock, birch and jack pine – are blooming now, pale pink. In the sunrise they look like big round snowdrifts against the dark foliage of evergreens. There should be ripe apples sometime in July.

Meanwhile, I eke out my supplies as well as possible. Still have canned beans, rice, a little peanut butter, though I've run out of crackers; powdered eggs and coffee that I'm trying very hard to like without milk. I fantasize about fresh bread and marmalade, mashed potatoes and butter. If it's this hard in spring, what will I do in winter? Starve to death - ?

I didn't think that far. But I know I'm never going back. What if Bruce comes looking for me? I'll hit him with my walking staff: two ribs - crack! crack! the sound of dry twigs. Or Mr. Reed, or my father – except I'd hit them on the head. If they tried to spoil this place for me, I'd be mad enough to hit them on the head. In the dream, most often Bruce comes by himself. I flatten him with a couple of whacks, loud ones, echoing. He lies on the ground, blood gushing from his nose, bewildered, helpless. He pleads and cries, swearing he'll be good. I wish I could believe it, but I know he won't change. I have to kill him then. Cut off his head with the hatchet – how many blows would it take, I wonder - and bury it far from his body, to make sure he stays dead. Unlike a kitchen floor, earth absorbs blood; I don't have to wash it up, afterward.

Who am I kidding? It's always women's bodies found in shallow graves. If Bruce caught up with me, I'd be learning, not him. That's what they call it: teaching you a lesson, you mouthy little bitch. Next day, you have to lie about the bruises, tell people you slipped on the stairs, but they mostly think you fell down drunk. Or they suspect the truth, nod sadly and avoid eye contact. I must be the dumbest person on Earth. You'd think after the first-class education Dad gave me, I would have been perfectly trained by the time I met Bruce.

~

I found a house! It must belong to somebody. If the owner returns, I'll have to vacate. But he hasn't used it in, looks like years. Nobody's lived here but wild animals that gathered twigs and leaves and wads of hay for nesting; left a pile of scat in the corner. It's all dried up and dusty; that animal is long gone. Nothing here now except mice and spiders. They'll just have to move over, because the new squatter is sweeping out the dirt, covering up the windows, like it or not. I'm sick of shivering in a pup-tent all night. Especially when it rains.

It's good construction, solid, built of logs. It's raised two steps off the ground, with a sturdy floor of rough-hewn board. The roof, of cedar slab and bark, doesn't leak; the wind doesn't blow through the walls. There is a stone fireplace at one end; the other end is partitioned off for two bunk beds. Somebody put this house together with thought and skill and hard work. What for?

Couldn't have been a settler: there's no cleared land and anyway it's not that old. A hunting lodge? Bruce used to go hunting with his buddies in deer season. He'd sell the venison to a specialty butcher shop. They must have stayed in a cabin like this one. No women allowed. Not that I wanted to go anyway, and now that I've seen deer close up, I hate the idea even more. How can anyone shoot something so elegant down in cold blood? With this wimpy attitude, I just might starve to death.

That could have happened to the owner. Or he might have been torn apart by wolves. I hear them at night, howling. Or maybe he killed himself. You read about men doing that, going off into the woods to do it. Maybe I'll stumble on his skeleton one day, leaned up against a tree, a rusty shotgun barrel wedged in his jaw, the back of his skull shattered. A manly way to go. Women are cowards; they take a jar of acetaminophen and wash it down with a bottle of vodka. Pain-killers. You're supposed to report human remains, but I wouldn't. Don't want policemen all over the place. Or any kind of men. I'd bury him, too. Might keep the shotgun... What for? I have no shells.

There's no outhouse; I dug a pit and tied saplings together, with cedar branches woven in horizontally, to make a sort of privy. Not that there is anyone to hide from. In three weeks, I haven't seen another human being, just animals. Lots of them. Squirrels, chipmunks, rabbits; a skunk the other evening strolled by without a care in the world, tail held jauntily high, like Pierre LePew in the old cartoons. And yesterday, a huge porcupine, sitting on a low branch, so still and quiet I almost walked right into him. Imagine getting a face full of quills! I really am stupid sometimes.

It's easier to wash my hair, now I've cut it short, but the stream is awfully cold. I'll be able to heat water in the cabin, once I clean out the fireplace and make sure no birds are nesting in the chimney. Birds are everywhere, nesting. I brought in plenty of firewood to dry; don't want smoke to alert anyone. I don't think there's anyone near enough to notice, but shouldn't get careless.

Sure could use some clean clothes! Must make a trip, anyway, before or my poor old car forgets how to run. Which way? Doesn't matter; any town will do. Have to buy kerosene for the lantern, a few more tools, a container to store rainwater; staple foods, soap - better make a list. Insect repellent – the black flies are fierce. Seeds? Plant a little vegetable garden, juts over there in the sunlit patch - yes. Still have enough money, if I'm careful.

I cancelled the credit cards, took what cash there was in our joint account – less than my share of the deposits. Bruce's cheques must be bouncing like tennis balls. Serves him right! Anyway, he got two months rent free, the electronics and the furniture. He's welcome to the sexy underwear and high heeled shoes he likes. I never did. I packed only practical clothes: pants, boots, sweaters, down jacket. Guess I must have expected to survive, after all. How? I have no skills.

Don't know what I expected. I wasn't thinking, really, just reacting. Like an amoeba in the experiment. Amoeba have no brain at all, yet they go toward things that are good for them - food, light, warmth - and go away from bad things, like pain. People often run toward things that will hurt them. I found Bruce and got lessons. My mother found my father, and was unteachable. They say women's brains are smaller than men's. But women still have bigger brains than other animals, and yet behave more stupidly than amoebas do with no brain at all - so that explains nothing. Except, amoebas have no sex; maybe that does. Well, I'm done with sex. I'm a hermit. I'll grow old alone, the Madwoman of North Nowhere. Celibacy is restful.

That's why all those crusaders retired to monasteries, after they were done with their campaigns, marauding and screwing around in foreign lands. Nuns probably joined a convent because it was the only way to get away from their fathers and not replace them with husbands. But if I'm honest – when you're all alone, there's no point in lying - I don't know if I could take the discipline and discomfort either of them endured willingly. They must have wanted something more – something about their soul.

I guess it's okay to think about souls when you live among ghosts, like it's okay to talk to them. Not only Muffin's spirit, either, which I've seen again, just last night. I wish I'd brought her here while she was alive to enjoy it. I talk to my mother, too, sometimes. I wish I'd talked to her more when she was alive. Or listened to her. I could have – I don't know – hugged her once in a while, given her support, made some gesture to show I understand. Maybe she wouldn't have left me. Only, I didn't understand. Still don't, not really, but I'm trying.

That's something you learn in the woods, to listen.

Listen: the wolves are calling again. Yipping from hilltop to hilltop, passing along a message, answering. Singing to one another, enjoying their weird harmonies. I should be afraid, but I'm not what they're after. In the city, it seemed I was everyone's natural prey. Here, I'm nobody's. I never knew how many kinds of sound animals can make. Listen: frogs in a pool: they croak, yes, but they're also chirping, honking, burping, buzzing and drumming. What have they got to talk so much about? Listen: a woodpecker hammering on a dry elm trunk. I've seen three different kinds. I wish I'd brought the bird book. Or any books, besides the field guide to edible plants. It's useful, but not very entertaining.

When I can't sleep, I listen, talk to ghosts, and sometimes light a candle to write in my notebook. Just for a little while.

~

There is a farm close by. I'd heard cattle lowing and followed the sound, over two densely wooded hills, across the stream where it's wide and deep enough to be grateful for high rubber boots; through some scrubby bush, into a field. There are ten cows and seven calves. They looked up from their grazing, considered, then started edging away, casual-like, as if the grass just happened to look greener, over that way.

Beyond the pasture, I could see a barn and the roof of a house. I went back to my camp, tidied up a bit and drove around by road, like a normal person. I practiced talking like one on the way. I used to be a good at customer relations, in another life, weeks ago. I must have done all right;

the woman at the farm didn't seem frightened or suspicious.

Her name is Betty. She's my mother's age – the age my mother would be. She's nice. Lonely, I think; her children, two boys and a girl, are grown and living so far away she rarely sees them. She sells brown eggs, which make a welcome change to field rations. Farmers are not allowed to sell unpasteurized milk, but she gave me a fill-up of my canteen for nothing. Oh, light brown coffee, what a luxury! I'll go back in a day or two, when I've thought of a credible story, and see if I can help with some chores, in exchange for fresh food.

I can work. I'm strong. I never knew that. The first couple of evenings, my arms cramped up quite badly, and my hands hurt, all blisters. It became easier, once I got the hang of holding a pitchfork correctly, lifting with my knees, not my back, never bending if I can stoop - There is a skill to everything, even the simplest task, like mixing compost or changing the straw in chicken coops. I work with Betty two or three hours weekday mornings, which leaves lots of time to dig in my own vegetable patch. This afternoon, I planted corn and pole beans, together, in hills. Legumes, that's what beans and peas are, replenish the soil that corn depletes, while using the corn stalk for support. What a good idea! My calluses are hardening up well, I like the feel of them, and so are my leg muscles and shoulders.

I saw that cat again, in the daytime. No ghost; it's
just an ordinary stray; a skinny calico with white
face and paws. She keeps her distance, but is
curious, too. I put out a bowl of milk last night and
it's gone – whether the little cat ate it or some
other animal, I don't know. She's a fitting first
subject for my brand new notebook from the small
department store where I buy sundries. Betty
suggested I take trips to the village on Saturday
morning, there are yard sales along the way,
where you can pick up tools and furniture,
blankets and curtains, for practically nothing.
There is a hardware store, too, and a bright,
cheerful one-room library close to the laundromat.
I can't join: even if I had a proper address, I
wouldn't give it out. But I can sit and study while
my clothes dry and they have a carousel of used
paperbacks for a quarter.

~

Today, I planted out a neat row of baby cabbages,
alongside a row of broccoli. I've been eating
lettuce and beet cullings, with wild rocket and
chickweed, for salad. Very nutritious, if a bit dull.
Peas are bushy and blooming, little tomato plants
look ambitious next to their tall stakes. I'm making
a fence of cedar posts intertwined with dogwood
and grape vine to keep the deer out. It should
work against rabbits, too, if only I can close the
gap soon – started collecting materials way too

late. They chewed my spinach down to the ground. Oh well; I'll plant more in the fall.

Today, I brought back a dozen jars of strawberry preserve: my wages for helping Betty pick and hull the berries, sterilize the jars. That's one more thing I know how to do. Peas will be next. She doesn't have much cash to spare and I'm happy to be paid in kind. Are you kidding? Heavenly preserves! Canned peas, dill beans and later on, beets, squash, apple-sauce, jam. She can use an extra pair of hands all through the season. The bedroom alcove will make a good pantry; the bunks are like deep shelves, and there's space for a water tank and wash-basin. In early spring, I liked my sleeping bag next to the fireplace. And though it's warm now, I still won't sleep where hunters may have left their violent dreams. Not that it's much of a problem these nights: I fall asleep too tired even to have my own.

I see the deer almost every morning. Five of them, three does and two fawns. I like to think one is the baby from that first magical sighting. It's not all sticks and knobs and spots anymore, but growing sleek and beautiful. They don't bound away: they stop, turn their heads in unison, their deep, lovely dark eyes assessing, not afraid. I don't threaten them; don't smell of whiskey and gunpowder. They stand like statues and stare for a moment, then stroll off among trees, going about deer business, life business: seeking fodder and shelter.

~

I stayed for lunch today, after bread-baking, and met Gus, Betty's husband. An angular, brown, quiet man. He occupies space like he belongs in it and it belongs to him: calmly. The way they are together, not saying much, but she'll pat his shoulder as she leans over to put a dish of stew on the table; he'll lay a big square palm on her hip, passing on his way to the sink. It's a pattern made of many years with a familiar partner. I was never like that with Bruce, never so easy and relaxed. My parents were never like that: I remember tension, not comfort. I cried a bit, after I got home.

Two funny things, reading over that sentence.

One is: I haven't cried for a long, long time. Not in Emergency, getting my ribs taped up – and that hurt. Not when Muffin's died, nor at her secret funeral. Not when I decided, finally, to leave Bruce. I thought, after my mother's suicide, I might never cry for anyone again. But it felt okay to shed a few tears over the Smiths. It's not envy – well, maybe a little – it's more like relief that they exist, that a durable, happy love exists. Their sons and daughter must have the kind of memories everyone should have of childhood.

The other funny thing is the word 'home'. This cabin is my home. The Smith boys built it, with their 4H friends, years ago. Nobody's used it since Ted moved to California and James went west to the oil fields. He and his new wife may be coming for Christmas. Anyway, I can stay as long as I want. Nobody's ever hunted here: the whole wood-lot is posted. I have a table now, with only one broken leg that I can replace, a kitchen chair, two rugs, a shelf for my books and wind-up radio. I made a bed of cedar and grapevine and started an armchair.

I've been learning from a library book, how to weave baskets and wreaths from willow branches, pine slat, dogwood boughs, marsh grass and all kinds of natural vegetation. Furniture is more complicated, but I have a knack; I can figure it out. Who knows, next summer I might be able to sell rustic wear at the farmer's market. Gus sells firewood by the cord and hires help on weekends, stacking and loading; I can earn some cash all winter, too. Better buy snowshoes so I can walk to work. Ha-ha!

Will I ever get a regular job, in a bank or someplace, and rent a normal apartment in a normal town? Maybe - someday.

Summer is almost over; there's a long pause between day and night. It's a busy time. The larder is filling up with jars and hanging sacks, even a braid of smooth little wild garlic bulbs. I like to stand in the curtained doorway, looking at my hoard, feeling competent and secure. Sometimes I have dinner with Betty and Gus; I take my mending, because it's easier by electric light, and we watch a television show. She never did ask about my past; I never needed that story – the truth was so much easier to tell.

Nights are restful and empty. I hope Bruce found someone to share his bed – someone smarter and braver than me, who can defend herself. I haven't started awake or had a dream about hurting and killing, since the tomatoes started to ripen. We made way too much sauce. Rabbits got the second planting of spinach and most of the cabbage. I'm not that fond of cabbage anyway. Raccoons stole some corn, but I left enough for me. I'm learning to share.

 It's hard to think in weeks and months out here: you count time in the progress of crops, in the colour of leaves, in the temperature of air in the morning, in chores finished and chores standing in line, waiting to be done. Cut willow branches. Pick plums. Make jam. Ask Gus for a few bales of straw to stuff under the floor for insulation. I don't care if mice nest in it, so long as they stay out of my house. They will: I put a bowl of food out every evening for the calico cat. We play hide and seek. I speak to her; she flattens her ears and skitters away into the shadows – not as fast or as far as she did yesterday.

Before the snow flies, before the bad dreams come again, she'll be in here, curled up by my feet.

Premonitions
by Francis Mont

Bratso, I am worried about my grandchildren. I don't see them as often as I would like to. As you know, my son and I don't get along very well, but, when he brings his kids for a visit, they light up my day. They are at the age when they start being curious about the world.

I had a really enjoyable discussion with Jennifer that time.

"Grandpops, how big is the world?" she asked.

They both call me that, after their father's ill advised joke of a salutation.

"Jennifer, do you know how long one kilometer is?"

"Yes, it's the same as a walk from our house to the library"

"Do you know how big a number forty thousand is?"

"I know: it is VERY BIG" she said with her cute little smile.

"Well, think of it this way" I said. You know that there are 24 hours in each day, 60 minutes in each hour and 60 seconds in each minute. That means that there are 86,400 seconds in each day.

That is a bit more than twice the forty thousand I asked you about"

"Are you still with me, Jenn?"

"Yes, I am – I told you it was very big!"

"OK, good"

"Now if you could walk from your house to the library in one second..."

Jennifer giggled. "Then I would be superwoman!".

"Then, it would take you a whole day, from early morning to late night to walk around the Earth".

"Wow! Earth is that big?"

"Yes, Jennifer, it's big enough".

I love their questions because, through their eyes, I can relive the wondrous discoveries I made myself in the remote past. Simon was 6, Sara was 7 and I was 71 last time they were here. You may not agree, but they think I am ancient and refer to the pictures in my photo album as antiques.

It's hard not to worry about them when you hear the news. I tried to talk to John about it, only once. "Pops, you are becoming a senile old fool!" he said. "You are so out of it, living in the boonies, without an occupation to keep your mind active. You don't have any friends to keep you sane, so you see dangers everywhere."

You see, Bratso, he's an engineer who believes that everything is fixable. His favourite mantra is: "Every problem has a solution and the human mind is an inexhaustible resource". He sees nothing wrong with blasting full speed ahead, in every direction, taking advantage of every opportunity. He doesn't know, or doesn't care, about the collateral damage. You and I know better. We see the dwindling songbird population, the disappearing bees, insects, frogs and garden snakes. We can't help noticing the crazy and unpredictable weather.

I have to agree with him about one thing: it would be nice to have close friends to share ideas, thoughts with, but I live out here, the nearest neighbor is 4 km away, it's hard to keep in touch. Still, I'm not as uninformed, as John thinks, I read a lot, follow the news and, as a scientist, I can connect the dots.

I see the trends in climate change, in the resurgence of racial hatred and in the sudden popularity of unscrupulous politicians who ride this new wave of intolerance.

When I tried to show John where these trends would lead, he laughed at me:

"Pops, you expect man-made disaster to hit us any minute! You never change, it's in your alarmist, conspiracy-theorist DNA. See why I don't visit more often? Frankly, it bores me to death to sit here with nothing to do but listen to your Armageddon predictions. I hope you are not poisoning my kids' minds with all that nonsense?"

I never tried again. And no, I'm not scaring my grandchildren about their future prospects. Let them enjoy their lives today, as long as today lasts.

I keep busy in my greenhouse, talking to my plants and to you, while I potter in moist soil. You think that I provided all these wonderful cat boxes just for you to play in. How many times do I need to tell you that tomatoes don't grow in cat piss?

Unlike you carnivores, I don't need meat, so I grow what I eat. Remember, when I had the solar system installed, I told you that we would be fully self-sufficient now? We have our water well, a stocked root cellar and freezer. We could survive here without outside help for months if necessary. I hope it won't come to that, but I think it's good to be prepared for anything that might happen."

It's climate change that worries me most. All the reports I have been reading from reputable scientists predict that the start of the runaway warming will be very sudden and it will quickly grow into a major catastrophe.

The food crises will come first – it takes only one major crop failure around the world to empty the shelves in grocery stores. I remember from my childhood in post war Europe, the endless standing in lines for basic necessities like bread and milk and eggs, if any left. I try my best to be prepared, not just for me but for my grandchildren as well. They live in a condo, on the top floor of a high rise, they have nowhere to go when it happens.

So I grow more than I can eat. For now, I donate the surplus to shelters when I drive into town for supplies.

~

You couldn't help noticing: we had a big fight then, John and I, their last visit, because I asked him to leave his kids here for summer vacation. I told him it could be a great help for a single parent, not having to hire baby sitters all the time. I thought I could teach them to love the country: plants, animals, gardening. It would do them good to be out of an apartment for a few weeks and you and I wouldn't be so lonely.

He laughed at me.

"Pops, you must be kidding – I wouldn't leave them here for a day without supervision. You would scare them to death with your crazy ideas. The last thing I need is a couple of screwed up kids. My job is important, I need to be able to concentrate on it, not to deal with my kids freaking out."

We had some words then, and I regret some of the things I said to him, but we both lost our tempers.

That was almost three years ago. I'm too proud to try again and he's too busy to call. Still, I'm here if they need me.

~

I don't listen to the news any more, it's too painful to see the world falling apart out there, claiming innocent victims in greater and greater numbers. The food riots have started, gas pumps are mostly out of fuel, random violence and organized crime are everywhere. The government tries to cope, I expect martial law to be declared any day now.

Finally, I couldn't stand another sleepless night, so I tried to call them on the phone, but his mobile was out of service and I couldn't leave a message.

I fear the worst.

I hope they remember me when they can't survive any more in the city. The roads are not safe, more and more armed gangs are ambushing escapees as they try to flee the city toward some distant sanctuary, places like my little oasis in the middle of nowhere.

I hope they remember and he drives very carefully on their way here.

Any day now.

I'll keep the porch light on for them – it's hard to find my place in the dark.

Terror on Cherry Street

by Vera Mont

Sarah Johnson loved the wide staircase, deep closets, high ceilings and low price. True, the house needed much renovation, but with both her and Richard's careers taking off, there would be more money coming in. True, the neighbourhood was run-down; peeling facades and rusting cars... But two homes had already been rescued by professional couples, and if the trend continued, the Johnsons' investment could easily double in four years. By the time their first child was born, they might be able to trade up to Markham.

For the interim, Cherry Street would suit them well enough. It had more than its share of seniors, apt to make a social event of sweeping their walkway or going to the convenience store. One old-timer who had taken root on his veranda never failed to disconcert Sarah, with a hearty "Hi, Beautiful!" and a grin too full of stained denture. The elderly occupied seedy rooming-houses or lived with married daughters – heavy, shapeless women with plastic shopping bags surgically grafted to their arms – and numerous offspring. Sarah had no intention of raising her babies (a boy and girl, three years apart) among the youngsters she saw, at all hours, playing ball, wrestling their dogs, squabbling, chalking grids on the sidewalk, pairing off, sometimes even eating, in the street. Nor was she pleased about the unemployed men with insolent eyes, who had nothing better to occupy their time than beer and endless card-games on their front porches.

Sarah had that outmoded feature replaced with wide, shallow steps of dark-stained spruce, with earthenware pots of azalea at each end. After the plate-glass window was installed, Richard hired a landscaping firm to dig up the climbing rose and forsythia roots and scrubby lawn. They put in a meandering walk of aged brick to match the freshly-scoured walls and covered the front yard in bark mulch, then planted tasteful islands of holly and yew shrub. By mid-June, the Johnsons recovered enough financially to construct a deck in the privacy of their back garden, and felt ready to begin entertaining.

They made friends with the neighbours. That is, they gave and were given drinks and canapes of a Friday evening. The Tremains – Julian, a resident in cardiology at the General, and Alyson, an insurance adjuster – were of the Johnsons' cohort, lively and fun. Geoffrey Bonard, though he lectured at the university, was not a bit stuffy; his partner, Stewart Prentice was an interiors consultant; generous with advice. They owned some marvellous antiques and their ivy-covered front garden had the most charming bronze fountain, complete with verdigris.

The Johnsons debated throwing a dinner party, but were not sure how the new acquaintances would mix with Richard's colleagues at the bank, and held off. After all, this was not to be their permanent abode. Still, they were tempted when the people who bought the splendid Victorian across the street finally moved in after a legal hassle with the sitting tenants. He was something big in mutual funds; might be useful to know. She managed a fabric design studio and had exquisite style. They were a few years older and had children. The sight of little Rebecca and tiny Reuben, adorable in matching SmalFolx rompers, being trundled off to play-school by their nanny, turned Sarah all gooey inside; almost made her want to accelerate her own baby schedule.

The Seimans had their weedy front yard scraped away, loads and loads of white sand delivered and raked in Zen patterns around three enormous tufa rocks. So dramatic! Alyson Tremain was pale and tight-lipped with envy: *her* imagination had to run to no more than bluegrass, weeping junipers and weathered cedar rail. The Seimans replaced their deep covered porch with a staggered three-tier bleached wood patio that must have cost ten times as much as the Johnsons'. Their new front door was a seamless teak plank – more elegant than the Tremains' mullioned glass; nearly as fine as the one Stewart Pentice had "picked up for a song" (everyone knew he paid a small fortune) from a demolished 18th century church.

Sarah now started her work-day by admiring the Seimans' front door on her way to the bus stop. In her next house – not here, that would be too obvious an imitation - she might get one like it.

One morning, she stepped outside as usual, glanced across the street – and nearly fainted. On the Seiman's beautiful teak door was spray-painted a huge, sloppy, shocking purple Z! More purple blots defaced the tufa rocks. It was horrible. What sick, perverted individual could do such a thing? Naturally, the police were called. They asked questions, took notes, walked around scratching their ears and backsides. No action resulted, and Mr. Sieman wondered aloud whether they took the incident seriously.

The following night, Sarah and Richard were startled awake by gun-shots. They we quite sure: two loud reports, then silence. The police, arriving with commendable despatch, found two beer bottles broken against the kerb. Neither the Seimans nor the Johnsons were satisfied with this explanation. Worse yet, the next night, when they were once again woken by gun-fire, the cruiser didn't come for a full fifteen minutes, and then the constable – a lone constable, with downy cheeks! – said it was most likely cherry-bombs. Firecrackers. In *June*?

That same week, the Tremains' rustic fence was covered with obscenities – words barely legible on the rough cedar; but their mere existence was obscene enough. Geoffrey and Stewart's fieldstone driveway was spattered with disgusting gobs of tar. Some truly destructive element was loose on Cherry Street. Sarah lugged her azaleas indoors for the night, and fretted about her hollies. She need not have: it was Julian Tremain's perfect blue lawn that began to die in a pattern of Z's. It had been sprayed with Killex.

Sarah no longer liked to walk up from the corner by herself, even in daylight. After dark, even with Richard beside her, she peered anxiously into each shadow, started at every noise. Nor would Julian Tremain let Alyson go anywhere alone. Geoffrey and Stewart both drove to work, so their routine was little disrupted, and the Seimans preferred entertaining at home to going out. During one of their more elaborate soirees (to which the Johnsons had not been invited – nor had any of the neighbours, so that was all right), every guest's car had a tire deflated and its windshield thickly smeared with petroleum jelly. The vandalism had been carried out with such speed, silence and precision, the perpetrators must have been highly organized.

A street- gang? Next, there would be drug-dealing, prostitution, burglaries… Sarah tentatively broached the subject of moving away.

"But, after all," Richard said, in the cool, reasonable tone she lately found rather more irritating than reassuring, "no-one's been hurt. It's just teenagers playing childish pranks. Anyway, nothing's been done to us."

This was true. Sarah wondered whether the fact was remarked by the victims, and according to what criteria the victims were picked. Prejudice might explain the attacks on the Seimans and the gay couple, but what of the Tremains? What set *them* apart from the Johnsons?

"These kids," Richard was still holding forth, "are uneducated. They have a low tolerance for change. They lash out at anyone they see as different or – well, frankly, more accomplished. Anyway, they'll be gone pretty soon, that will put an end to the vandalism."

Sarah was unconvinced. How did he know? How could he be so sure that vandalism wouldn't escalate into terrorism?

Richard continued, "Have you noticed how many homes on this street are on the market? Number eighteen's just been sold."

"What's that got to do with anything?" Sarah asked pettishly.

"It went for $25,000 more than we paid, and the lot's smaller."

Sarah was amazed. They never dreamed it would happen so fast.

"The realtors have caught on. They're soliciting potential sellers, promising them very attractive prices. Property taxes will keep rising," said Richard, sounding less insufferable and making more sense, "along with property values. More motivation for people to vacate, don't you think? Our investment will double in a couple of years."

To Sarah, this meant they'd be able to start the first baby sooner; motivation to hang on, though she was still nervous. In fact, three more extended families moved out in the next month. Richard was proved right. But Sarah was right, too, because the spray-painting got worse. Purple Z`s appeared on house walls, windows, sun-decks. Cherry bombs – if that`s all they were – disturbed everyone`s sleep almost nightly.

The Seimans' wonderful, exotic front garden was used for unmentionable purposes. Their nanny quit. The Seimans considered moving to Forest Hill, but had too much sunk in the house. Instead, they imported a girl from Haiti who was fearless and spoke fluent French. The Tremains replaced their ruined lawn with hardy sweet fern – which harmonized better with juniper, actually - and their glass front door with a brushed steel one – almost as smart, though it made the hall rather dismal. The couple who bought #18, George – only 34, and already a partner at his law firm – and Babs Stutska, began remodelling the inside; left their porch and picket fence untouched, for the time being.

Sarah and Richard, inexplicably immune from persecution, nevertheless joined their neighbours in demanding a strong police presence. They were still awaiting a response the night K'ung F'u, Geoffrey Bonard's prize Pekingese, failed to return from his pre-bedtime constitutional. Geoffrey went up and down the street with a flashlight, calling, in vain. When he came back to enlist Stewart's assistance in the search, he found their bronze fountain overturned, its peeing cherub broken off at the ankles. The dog showed up next morning, unharmed; there was no evidence to support Geoffrey's conviction that he had been kidnapped. The fountain, however, cost a fair piece of change to repair and was gone for weeks....

... During which, nothing happened. Nothing at all. Sarah felt uneasy about this sudden calm. Was a storm on its way? What were the vandals plotting? What new, outrageous act of destruction was to follow? The answer came from Alyson Tremain, predictably – God only knew how, but Alyson always got wind of things before anyone else.

"The house on the corner's up for sale," she reported. "The awful little clapboard with the sagging porch?" Sarah could not see why this news should cause such excitement, yet Alyson was fair bursting with it.

"Not much can be done with that eyesore," she mused, "but the corner lot's nice. Maybe they'll bulldoze it and ..."

Alyson interrupted, "That's not the point! The *reason* it's for sale is, the old man passed away."

"The one with yellow dentures, smiling all the time?" Sarah wasn't sure whether to be sorry or relieved. "When? How?"

"Three weeks ago. Heart attack. Must have been Stewart's fountain that did it." Alyson paused to build suspense, so smug with secret knowledge, Sarah refused to ask. "Guess what they found in his house!"

"Cockroaches? He didn't look too clean. Don't tell me we'll have to fumigate?"

"No, no, nothing like that," Alyson began to sound exasperated. "They found purple spray-paint, cans and cans of it. Firecrackers, and tar and weed-killer. Empty Vaseline jars. Don't you get it? *He* was the terrorist!"

That bent, skinny old man? All by himself? Yes, it seemed so, because there were no further incidents.

Within a week, the property was snapped up by an architect – divorced, but the right age for Richard's sister, and not too bad looking. He had the outside walls done over in palest cream stucco, the sagging porch replaced with a full façade of Spanish arches, the roof re-covered and the driveway paved in burnt umber tile, the yard planted with Russian sage and yucca and fenced with wrought iron. Sarah could hardly wait to see the inside.

Amazing, what an imaginative person can do for a house! What a dozen such people can do for a street.

House Arrest

By Francis Mont

It happened this morning, without much fanfare: when I tried to go for my usual run, I couldn't get out. I got the real surprise when I called the superintendent and he said he was locked in too. I called every number in my address book and it was the same. I knew that curfew violators were locked in by the robots, but this time it seemed to be *everybody*.

What had happened? I turned on the TV. Every channel I tried kept repeating the same announcement: until further notice, the whole town is under house arrest. Food will be delivered by robots, medical emergencies will be responded to by mechanised medical teams, communication channels will remain open, but no human will be allowed outside their domicile.

I called Martha again, after I had talked to everyone else. Martha is my girlfriend. She lives in the same apartment building, two floors above me. She's a terrific painter, mostly in watercolour, though she occasionally ventures into acrylic. I could hear from her voice that she was scared.

"Trevor, what's going on? Why are we locked in? What's going to happen?" Her voice broke on a pathetic little sob.

"I don't know, but maybe Big Brain decided we needed some time to cool down. Things have been pretty wild lately."

"Yes, but how long will it last? When will we get out?"

"I don't know, Martha, all I know is what the TV told me and I am sure you watched the same announcement."

"Yes, I have and it was so cold, so impersonal, so *inhuman*!"

"I agree. Maybe it was a mistake to entrust the administration to computers and robots, but we had no choice!"

"I remember," Martha sounded a bit more in control of her voice now. "The economy was falling to pieces before the computers took over and, since then, it's been running smoothly."

"One problem solved, another created," I couldn't help being philosophical in spite of our alarming predicament. "Once the computers and the robots took care of everything, we became superfluous, without a purpose, without a place to belong."

"That never happened to me," Martha objected. "I've been an artist all my life and that didn't change with the stupid robots running things!"

"That's true," I agreed. "But the rest of us weren't so lucky. I have no job anymore, let alone a career. What can I do that a robot can't do better?" The memory of being humiliated by clever machines still rankled.

"Lots of things!" Martha tried to be supportive. "Your wood carving is coming along, and your stories are more entertaining every day."

"I know we're OK, but most people couldn't adjust very well. They are bored out of their minds, trying to find some excitement in street fighting and random destruction."

"That must be why the robots locked us in," Martha concluded. "But how long will it last? If only you'd been sleeping over, at least we could keep each other company, but now we're stuck in separate units!" She started to cry.

"We have to find a way to get together." I agreed. "I would like to be with you too, and not just for …you know."

"I can't even think of sex right now Trevor, I'm too worried and too angry. You're the engineer. Can't you find a way to unlock our doors?"

"I will try, Martha. I'll call a few of my old colleagues to see if we can come up with any ideas. I will get back to you once I know something."

~

Deep in the underground complex, a powerful mind was considering its options. It knew that the interim solution wouldn't last. It needed to find a permanent resolution to the crisis. Its programming was unalterable: to do everything in its power to keep humanity safe and comfortable.

Keeping them safe was easy enough: their physical needs were taken care of by automated factories. They had shelter, food, medical service, education, communication and entertainment. They did not need to work for a living; they were free to spend their days any way they wished.

Yet, judging by their destructive behaviour, they were not happy. Street fights, vandalism and random violence were on the rise; the number of suicides increased daily.

Locking them in was a necessary step and it was simple to achieve. The general curfew had been in place for months: all citizens were in their apartment units by 2200 hours; all it needed to do was throw a switch and lock all doors simultaneously.

Nobody lived in detached houses any more: for optimal use of material and energy resources, cities had been converted to high-rise blocks, equipped to provide all necessary services.

Nobody lived in the countryside: with large-scale hydroponic factory food production, livestock and fields were no longer required. The obsolete farms had been abandoned and depopulated.

There was no government, as such: distribution and servicing were supervised by the computers, carried out by robots. Humans were mostly left alone to regulate their own affairs, resolve their own disputes.

Not everybody was unhappy in the system: according to reliable data, many citizens never left their units for months and even years, spending their entire time indoors, immersed in the unlimited entertainment options available on their 3-D viewers, in their sampling of chemical substances, in sexual adventures with human or virtual partners.

The troublemakers were a different story.

Anything could trigger an outburst: jealousy, rivalry over sports teams, an accusation of theft, even an accidental bump on the street could erupt into a fistfight that quickly degenerated into a mob scene: everyone fighting everyone else.

~

I never got the door open. I had nothing to work with: the era of handymen fixing things was long gone. The delicate woodcarving tools I used weren't up to the job. I couldn't even break the solid hard plastic by banging heavy pieces of furniture against it. All I managed was to exhaust myself with no gain. I had to think it over before calling Martha again.

If I couldn't open the door myself, could I, somehow, make the robots open it for me? The announcement on TV gave me an idea for one option: to fake a medical emergency. The medical unit would arrive, open the door and... then? They'd discover quickly enough that I'm not sick or injured. I couldn't expect to run past them, out to the corridor. Where would I go anyway? I'd be caught and returned before I reached the lobby.

What if we created a mass emergency? Wouldn't it overwhelm the robots? Maybe even the central computer? Communication lines were open; we were free to organize. It could be done in a short time, if I called all my friends and they called all their friends. At a prearranged moment, we would all report a heart attack. It should be coordinated precisely; the alarm had to be absolutely simultaneous. Pretending to be more confident than I felt, I called Martha and told her my plan.

~

The Great Mind in Central Plexus was alerted to the report of a citywide outbreak of heart attacks. A very quick calculation showed the probability of such an event astronomically small: zero for all practical purposes. The only other possible explanation was an organized rebellion by the humans. It did not take long to trace the calls from the communication logs back to the block and unit of origin.

This situation had to be dealt with, before it escalated into a serious drain on the city's resources. TGM activated its communication channel to Apartment B35/42/171.

~

I was resting after the med-bot left, having assured me that I was in perfect health, when the priority com-link came alive with a pleasant male voice that I had heard before. It was the voice of the Central Plexus computer.

"Citizen Trevor Dubois, I think you know who I am and what I am calling about."

It sounded friendly, soothing.

"Yes, I know who you are, or rather what you are," I answered, somewhat defiantly, trying to present a more confident mood than what I was in.

"I know what you did, Trevor, and I think I know why, but I am not sure what we can do to resolve this. Do you have a suggestion?"

I was flabbergasted. I had not thought of any solution before starting this protest; my immediate aim had been simply to regain our freedom.

"I know what I want – to be let out!" I almost shouted at the stupid machine, for not seeing the obvious.

"You want me to let you out? How would it solve anything? What would you do outside all by yourself?"

This was the literal mind of the computer that always irritated me. What was I going to tell him? Let everybody out? That wouldn't be a good idea – we would be back at square one. Some people are safe to let loose, some are dangerous. How to decide who should be free and who shouldn't?

"I have to think about this" I told it. "Can I call you back?"

"Just pick up the receiver when you are ready, I will know and we can talk again."

The com-link went dead and I was alone in my room to ponder.

~

My cogitation was interrupted by the buzzer indicating an incoming call. It was Martha. I was pleased that she called because my brain was ready to explode from fruitless searching for a solution. The problem was the complexity: not one single cause could be identified that would require one single solution..

"It didn't work!" she wailed. "The med-bot told me I was OK and didn't even let me join you! What are we going to do now?"

"You won't guess who called me a little while ago. I'll tell you because you can't possibly imagine! I know I couldn't. The Big Brain itself! It figured out the whole plot and traced the calls from the network logs back to me."

"Oh my God, Trevor, are you in trouble?"

"You won't believe it! It wanted my advice on how to resolve this situation."

"So, what did you answer?"

"I told its highness that I needed to think and I would call it back."

"Just like that? How will you contact it?"

"It told me to pick up the receiver and ask for the Central Plexus."

"You mean it's listening to the com-lines? It can hear everything we say to each other? This is scary, Trevor, I don't like to be so close to that freak!"

"I don't think it listens to this line unless I ask for it specifically, so you can relax for now. We need to decide what to tell it when I call back."

"Simple. We want to get out of here."

"Go back to the anarchy we had before? I don't think you'd like that!"

"What else can we say, Trevor?"

"I have an idea, and I want to discuss it with you and all our close friends. Big Brain just might act on my suggestion and I don't want to be personally responsible for the outcome. Not without consulting as many of our friends as I can reach."

"Go ahead, Trevor, I have all the time in the world." she sounded bitter and I couldn't blame her.

"We have to go back, at least in mind, to the past, before the problems started. People were much more sensible as long as they had useful occupations, when they had a place in society and could contribute to their own welfare. Sure, we had problems then too, but we knew what they were. The economy was run down by the greedy bastards who wanted all to themselves and while they were getting richer and richer, the rest of us were more and more marginalized. So we fought back, went on strikes, refused to co-operate. The economy suffered and the robots and Big Brain took over and things settled down. Except people were cut out of the production process and thus became redundant, superfluous, useless parasites. And, it turned out even worse."

"I can't disagree with you, Trevor, but what can we do? It seems to me that we can't go back and we can't stay here."

"I think it needs a multi-faceted solution. No single silver bullet will solve our problem."

"OK, how many bullets are you talking about? What are they like in concrete suggestions?"

"What gave me an idea is the fact that not everybody is unhappy now. You know, what Larry Niven called the 'wireheads'?

"Never heard of it." Martha wasn't a science fiction fan.

"Those who never left their apartments, even before we were locked in. The junkies, who are totally oblivious to life outside of their entertainment center? They are as happy as they want to be. The robots provide for all their needs."

"So, how does that lead to a solution?"

"By itself it doesn't, but it started me thinking."

Martha was chuckling now. "At least it accomplished something for a change! So what grand conclusions did it drive you to?"

"It started me thinking about different kinds of people and I realized that there are basically three types. Those that I just called 'wireheads'; those who are happy as long as they have a productive role in society, and those who are risk takers, adventurers, the kind that value their freedom and independence over everything else. This last group includes inventors, explorers, artists, writers and, of course, the criminals."

"Thank you for including me in this anointed group. I'm honoured, although I don't like to be grouped together with criminals, but I see your point. I hope you count yourself in with us, so we can stay together!"

"Absolutely, you can be sure of that. Based on this analysis, we don't need one suggestion, but three - one for each type of people."

"You mean to let the 'wireheads' be; give the majority some meaningful role and let us risk-takers be free to do what we want? Except for the criminals, of course. Is that it?"

"Almost, and I know it would suit you, but it wouldn't work for me personally."

"Why not? Don't you want to be free?"

"Of course I want to be free, but I can't be an engineer any more. I couldn't do anything that Big Brain and the robots wouldn't do better! I have to be realistic about it."

"You have your wood carving and writing now, Trevor, and you are getting better all the time!"

"Martha, I'm no great talent and I know my limitations. This was nothing more than a hobby to help keep me sane, to have something to do. It doesn't make me happy the way painting does you."

"So, what would you want, if you could do anything?"

"I may finally have an answer. I always dreamed about being a pioneer, even as a child, and never had a chance to fulfill that fantasy."

"What do you mean a pioneer?"

"I was thinking about all those abandoned farms outside the cities, out in the country where nobody lives any more. If the robots let me out, I want to go there, find the remnants of a small family farm and try to restart it. If I could live on what I grow, I would be independent, productive. It could be the biggest challenge and adventure of my life. That's something I can get excited about, and I can't be the only one who feels this way."

"Wow! Trevor, this sounds scary. You are an engineer, you don't know anything about farming!"

"I can learn, Martha. There are books and videos and I'm sure Big Brain could help with advice and the material I would need. If I convinced it that this would make me happy. After all, that's the objective of its programming".

"And what about us?"

"You could come with me, Martha, You could paint anywhere in the world. Think of the new subjects, the landscape! I'd protect you and make you comfortable."

"I don't know, Trevor, I have to think about this. Let's talk to others and see if anybody else wants to join us. If there were others around, to deal with all kinds of emergencies we can't even think of now, this idea would not be so frightening."

"Do you mean that you might consider this life with me?"

"I would always consider anything that could make you happy, you should know that. That's what love means, Trevor."

"I love you too, Martha. Let's make this work!"

Birthday

by Vera Mont

Her vague sense of oppression was too familiar to require close examination – until Young Frank arrived, bearing gifts, and then it had a name: aging. Maggie was turning thirty-eight on Monday. Her nephew delivered a bouquet of white carnations on behalf of his father, a big box of chocolates from his grandfather, Elder Frank, and a message from his mother: "Tell Dave 6:30 so you can get here by 7."

They were like that, the Hoyles: thoughtful and generous. You could be overwhelmed by them, especially all in the same room, in celebratory mode, as they would be tonight. One could drown in kindness. No, that was unfair. She must not rain on Cecile's parade. The guest of honour would look her best, be charming and appropriately gratified. To cheer up, she opened the box and carefully selected a bon-bon. She might even permit herself a second one after lunch.

Drawn by his infallible sugar-sensor, like a hummingbird to nectar, came the last of the Hoyle men, wearing his cap indoors as usual, slouching in that way he'd been cultivating of late, presumably to drive his mother crazy.

"Hiya, Toots, whazzup?" He swooped down on the box in Maggie's lap. "Candy! Betcha they're from Grandpop," Rob's cheeks puffed out, his knees spread apart and abdomen protruded, for a fraction of a second graphically impersonating Elder Frank.

"Go ahead," Maggie said, conscious and feeling just a bit guilty that the bribe was intended to get rid of him.

The boy snatched up a large square piece and bit into it. "Caramel. Yuch!" He deposited the uneaten portion in an ornamental enamelled dish, took a quick survey and made a second choice, which he stuffed into his mouth whole.

With determined precision, Maggie replaced the lid and held tightly the edges of the box. She said nothing. If she reprimanded him now, it might start one of the shouting-matches of which their relationship seems to consist these days. And that would mean going to the party in hostile silence. Not worth it.

"Thanks, Toots," Rob called back cheerfully as he sloped off, pulling the horrible denim cap down over his eyes.

It's so unfair, Maggie thought. They start out so sweet and helpless. By the time they turn into monsters, you've invested too much love and effort; and they've got your eyes or chin, you can't even disown them. The challenge is not to strangle him for three or four years – years! - until he metamorphoses into a human being. That's probably why boarding schools exist.

Robbie, who had recently stopped answering to that nickname, wanted only his hockey team at his tenth birthday, and he wanted them all taken to an arcade style restaurant. Maybe next year, Maggie had told him: she wasn't about to snub her in-laws without prior discussion. Young Frank, three years Rob's senior, didn't have family parties anymore. That must really hurt Cecile, who loved throwing them, but she still had a little girl. For Maggie, this would be the last children's party.

The presents were a predictable assortment of models, sport gear and an encyclopedia of snakes and lizards, Rob's all-consuming interest of the moment. As a consolation for putting up with his grandparents and cousins, Maggie surprised him with a piñata in the shape of a Mantella frog that she had made herself and decorated as realistically as possible with black, yellow and green crepe paper. He loved it. He promised not to tell everyone about the venom, but of course they would guess. He could hardly wait to demolish it. When the climax of the party finally arrived and candy spilled from the ruptured belly of the giant amphibian, everyone got into the spirit. Kids and adults alike went scrambling for the loot.

All except one. Rob's seven-year-old cousin, Karyn, looked on silently, with tears running down her pink cheeks.

"What's wrong, honey?" Maggie asked her. "Don't you want any candy?"

The little girl looked up at her. "He killed it. Robbie killed it!"

Maggie tried to explain the concept of the pinata. "You're supposed to break them, for good luck."

"But it was pretty. Why would you break something so pretty?"

Maggie experienced a pang of regret over the paper frog; a minor one for coming up with the idea in the first place, and major one for the daughter she never had. Both passed, and she hit upon a solution. She rescued the pinata's still intact head and gave it to Karyn, who turned it into a hand-puppet, and was happy.

Maggie rose heavily from the couch. Eight hours to go before the party and a hundred things to get done. With both Dave and herself working extra long days at this time of year, the maintenance and housekeeping always piled up for the weekend, leaving them little opportunity to relax or talk to each other. Not that they had any subject matter besides his problems with a contract, most of which Maggie didn't understand, or her frustrations with office politics, which didn't interest Dave. Once tax season and spring repairs were over, they must dedicate more time to family life…. Such as it was.

Sandwiches would do for lunch, since they were bound for an elaborate dinner. At this very moment, Cecile would already have made her house shine, and be humming like a well-oiled, contented little dynamo, cooking something gourmet, instructing Karyn in the intricacies of seasoning. Cecile was the consummate home-maker and parent, whom her sister-in-law admired without resentment – but never entirely untainted by envy.

Not that taking care of Maggie's own home was so awfully hard: it was efficiently laid out, modern and convenient. They had bought it brand new, customized to order, only ten years ago. At the time, they revelled in all the extra rooms, the sunny back yard, the wide patio. The second child they had planned never came, and now the house felt too big for three. Rob was engaged, it seemed, every evening, in extracurricular activities; on the weekend, he preferred the company of his peers. Somehow, he managed to keep up his grades. In three or four years, he would be off to college and the nest would be empty.

She pushed the vacuum cleaner around indifferently – there wasn't enough traffic in the living room to dirty the carpet - then attacked the dust. She always left polishing the sideboard for last: it was her favourite chore.

Dave conducted her into the dusty shop on Mill Street, and all the way back through the interior. There, up-ended between a hideous ornate armoire and a stack of unsorted chairs, was an ungainly piece of furniture, painted dark brown.

"That one?" Maggie regarded it with deep suspicion. "It doesn't look like much."

The grizzled proprietor took a belligerent stride forward, clutching his retro suspenders for effect. "That, young lady, is a genuwine antique. You won't find nothin' to touch it anywheres near the price."

Avoiding Dave's beseeching gaze, she squinted into the shadow. "Looks very hard-used. Scratched and crazed all over."

"That's nothing," the geezer insisted, "your old man here can easy touch up them little scrapes."

"No, it's just too big," Maggie stood firm. "And besides, eighty dollars is more than this month's budget can bear." At last, she did look directly at her husband. "I'm sorry."

"Fifty," said the old man, "and I'll even help load 'er up."

It was no mean feat, but eventually, the sideboard perched incongruously atop their compact car, criss-crossed with rope; the drawers crammed in the back seat with Robbie sulking between them. Maggie and Dave had giggle-fits all the way home.

It took her weeks to strip, sand and refinish the thing. Under two layers of paint and one of ancient varnish was solid walnut, constructed with dove-tailed precision. It was worth every minute, every broken nail, every skinned knuckle. Dave's eye for quality proved once again unerring.

They added some nice pieces later on, of sound provenance and at considerably higher prices. But this was the first fine thing in their new home, as they struggled to meet mortgage payments and made do with the shabby furnishings of their previous place. After a decade, it still gave her pleasure. Because one loves the work of one's hands? No: she didn't regret selling the little house on Elizabeth Street, every square inch of which had been scraped, patched, papered and painted by those same hands. They had never intended to stay there.

At a half past noon, Dave returned from an emergency inspection of his current project. The wrong gage of sewer pipes had been delivered; returning those had set the schedule back two full days. He was so intent on the problem of logistics, manpower allocation, overtime pay, that she hardly needed to respond. His preoccupation, however, did not detract from the single-minded dedication with which he fed himself.

"I was thinking," he said, reaching for a third sandwich, "about our vacation. Should we take Rob?"

Maggie, whose attention had wondered, registered the change of subject and tuned back in. The prospect of two unremitting weeks in the company of a grumpy, rude adolescent did not greatly appeal. She mentally scanned the family ledger for the price of sport or nature camp.

"Because," Dave continued, "I sort of feel we ought to spend time with him while we can. On the other hand, it would be nice to get away on our own."

The other hand, Maggie thought, sounds good. But, a nagging fear surfaced briefly, asking, "What if we discover we have nothing in common?"

Dave didn't look up at her lack of response; he was busy fishing for the last pickle in the jar. "I was thinking, we might want to go early this year. You look kind of beat lately."

If he says 'thinking' one more time, thought Maggie, I'll scream. What she said was, "You know I can't possibly get away before May. Anyway, Rob has school."

"Well, but, he could stay with Cecil and Stan. They wouldn't mind. Young Frank is starting an apprenticeship in Montreal next month. Rob might fill a void, sort of." The pickle continued to elude him and he kept doggedly after it. "That bright girl, What's-her-name, could take over some of your clients, couldn't she?"

Take over is just what Sophie was waiting for a chance to do. She'd told Dave about this concern before. "You know how busy tax season is. And then audits… "

He finally speared the pickle and held it aloft triumphantly. "I was just thinking, we should decide pretty soon."

She didn't scream. She said, "I'll think about it."

He had marched three carrot slices up into the mashed potato fort and now proceeded to sprinkle them with gravy. "Down came the RAIN and washed the spi-hi-ders out," he sang, as the carrots slid back onto his plate.

In Robbie's illustrated world, every fresh concept, each new-learned rhyme, had to take concrete form. Maggie expected him to make contact with aliens before he turned five.

"Out came the SUN," he bent, leering over his victims, "and dried up all the rain-and..." The words eluded Robbie, but never for long, "... the sree" triumphantly waving the correct number of chubby digits, "spi-ders ate all their meaf-loaf UP!" He regarded his mother with round blue eyes. "What did you learn at school today?"

"I don't go to school anymore, honey, I go to work."

Robbie pondered, shoving carrots around the base of his potato hill. "Daddy goes to work."

"Yes," Maggie said, "and now Mommy does, too. Eat your spiders, and maybe we'll have time to get the guitar out practice that song before Daddy gets home."

"Okay," said Robbie, then set about methodically squashing every carrot slice with his spoon before gobbling it with dramatic ferocity.

By 4:30, she had finished the dishes and laundry, tidied the kitchen and ironed some shirts, including the garish jungle print Rob had set his heart on for tonight, which was so ugly, Maggie couldn't help secretly admiring his chutzpa. Normally, this was the hour she started cooking dinner – with extra for the weeknights she would be home late. Today, she had a full two hours to get ready – an uncommon luxury. Time for a long, hot, scented bubble-bath to make up for the rushed early-morning showers.

Dave had retired to the den with a stack of accounts – uncomplaining for once. He hated bookkeeping. She, a professional, could do it in less than half the time… Yes, but she was so tired of financial statements by the weekend…. Well, why didn't she cut back on the work-load… Because someone more energetic would get the promotion… After all, it was his business; she didn't know the particulars … She could learn if she were interested… She already had a job… This Saturday, she almost missed the same old tired argument.

It always seems to be about work, not anything serious between us, she realized. There was no chance in the world of Dave being unfaithful; he seemed to lack the chromosome for deceit. Nor had he ever exhibited jealousy or suspicion as so many husbands do. They agreed on matters of child-rearing and liked each other's friends well enough. She didn't interfere in his business decisions, even when she considered them unwise; he left the family budgeting to Maggie and had learned to resisted impulsive purchases. At first, you have to worry constantly about money. By the time you're doing all right, it's become a habit you can't break. Do we need more?

Why do I want to be assistant head of the department? For the extra responsibility? So I can have more stress in my life? To keep checking over my shoulder if that little witch Sophie has got her knife out? I used to love accounting - the elegant purity of numbers; their absolute truth; the symmetry of a balanced ledger, the harmony. But I don't like my job. And, she realized with a shudder, I'm not all that crazy about my life. I just haven't had any time to notice.

It becomes the standard, this routine of small irritations, self-censoring and compromise. For both of us. What did it cost Dave to refrain from grumbling? Does he know I appreciate the effort? Does he appreciate the times I don't criticize or nag? Are we even?

Dave turned up the volume on the TV and poured them each a glass of sweet, cheap red wine. The people upstairs were fighting again: she was a sloven…. he was a boor… the kids were a pain in the ass… well, who kept having them…. well, who can't make a decent living to keep them in shoes… He swore; she cried; the children whined and cowered.

Dave said, "I've been thinking. We have some money saved,"

"Two thousand and seventy dollars." Maggie supplied automatically.

"My parents could spare maybe three,"

"Not easily!"

"But they wouldn't mind," he insisted, "and we really need to move out of here. It's depressing, and I've been thinking it might not be safe. If I take that job out west, I'll be gone all summer. Sure, the pay's good, but I just hate *the idea of you being here alone, with that," he rolled his round blue eyes toward the ceiling, "going on."*

Maggie stroked the back of his neck. "Don't worry. They only hurt each other. If it makes you feel better, I'll stay over on Friday nights after dinner with your folks. I'll be all right."

"Yes, but, listen. There are some good little fixer-uppers we could have right away for a minimal down payment."

"And that's what we'll get. As soon as we've saved enough on our own. I'll pick up some private work on the weekends to cover my last semester's tuition and have something left over. We can probably do it by next fall."

Dave shook his head doubtfully, but his eyes were already shining with the project far ahead, measuring lumber and laying tile.

"Besides," she said, inclining her chin upward, where the fight was sputtering to an exhausted impasse, "that's a reminder. We are never going to be like them."

"Never," he agreed fervently. "Not in a million years."

Nor had they. Their bouts of discontented bickering were always restrained and dignified compared to the anonymous upstairs neighbours of long ago. But just as inconclusive; just as devoid of real communication. It's tiring, yet nothing is resolved. So your encounters become predictable and short. The house finally achieved with so much shared effort becomes a terminal for arrivals and departures rather than a home. "Have you seen my note-case?" "You left it on the sideboard." "Thanks!" "Bye!" The long-awaited miracle child grows out of the age where everything he does is marvellous, and you drag your aching back home every night to: "How come you don't bake muffins anymore?" and "But *why* can't I have more snakes?"

The woman in the mirror, still young, had a decent figure – maybe even better than just decent. Her hair was a rich auburn; the few silver strands, invisible to the casual eye, though their owner knew she would have to start colouring in a year or two. In a few years, she thought, I might not care, I might too dull to start anything new. But for now, in the royal blue velvet sheath, she wasn't half bad. Maggie fastened her earrings, checked the contents of her evening bag.

"Do you need help buttoning the cuffs?" she asked Dave. She noted the strain on his belt, but didn't mention it.

He was a slow dresser at the best of times; on special occasions, it took him forever to comb his rebellious curls flat enough, to find the right socks, to choose the perfect tie. Even now, five candidates were draped precisely equidistant over a chair back. After a brief perusal, she chose the blue stripe, held it up in front of her dress to demonstrate the nearly perfect match. He smiled, nodded happily and put it on.

Rob stood in front of his closet, catatonic with indecision.

"What's the matter? Why aren't you dressed?" Maggie struggled to keep annoyance out of her voice.

"I can't find a shirt."

She glanced at the awful green leafy specimen now crumpled on his bed, and at its dozen varicoloured brethren hanging on the rod.

"Dad says I godda wear a tie, so that one's no good. A tie!" Rob repeated indignantly. "What happened to my brown shirt with white stripes?"

"It has a horrible great stain on it," answered his long-suffering mother, "Which, by the way, how did it get there?"

"Oh yeah. That idiot Cranshaw spilled iodine in Chem lab. It shoulda come out," he added accusingly.

"It didn't." Unable to contain her impatience, Maggie yanked out the least brightly coloured shirt in the closet and thrust it at her son. The hanger thudded on the carpet in her wake. "If you're not downstairs in ten minutes, you can walk. And wear a belt. Your pants are falling off."

She left him rooted to the spot, still catatonic, this time with shock. The twinge of guilt she felt was soon eclipsed by further irritation when she found Dave still combing his hair.

"Hurry up," she told him, "I'm warming the car."

She watched Dave run along the beach like a puppy let off the leash. He had insisted they push on to the coast: having come so far, it would have been a shame to miss the ocean, even if they could only spend one day here before turning for home. Emerging from the cool majestic indifference of the coastal mountain range, here it finally was: the Pacific Ocean spread before them in all its wide, bright, placid perfection. And Dave was revelling in the experience as only he could.

Now he stopped and picked up a pebble to lob across the surface of the water. It skipped twice before sinking with a splash. He chose the next pebble with care and did a little better. Much methodical searching and many attempts at last resulted in a seven-skip throw. He whooped with joy and leapt into the air, then performed the feat three more times, to prove it wasn't a fluke. That's my Davey, she thought.

His jeans were riding very low: Maggie just now realized how much weight he had lost in the last frantic months. Final exams, a part-time job and a spirited love-life might be too much even for Dave Hoyle's impressive stores of energy. He had earned this vacation and badly needed it. Who knew when they could afford another? Dave had a full-time job now, but her internship didn't start till September, and only at half starting salary. Though rent and car payments didn't leave much over, they were determined to put something into the house fund every month.

They had not splashed out on the wedding, but, by whatever gods may be, they deserved a proper honeymoon. Better make him put on a shirt, she thought, before he burns. In a minute…. Right now, it was too pleasant, watching his body in perpetual motion. She unpacked their picnic lunch and poured a small libation to the coastal gods and raised the thermos in a salute to her beautiful new husband.

Stan was the perfect host, as usual, taking coats, offering refills, paying compliments. He had gained probably five pounds since she had last seen him: Hoyle men tended to be athletic in youth and spread in middle age. Cecile wore a dress of her own design and execution, very chic and becoming. Elder Frank hugged the female guests a little bit longer than etiquette required, but he was so like Santa Claus that none of them minded. Maggie's friend Barbara sported a flamboyant new hairstyle and a new soccer-playing boyfriend. Alexis showed up uncharacteristically solo. Young Frank was gallant, handsome and attentive – a heart-throb in the final stages of training.

The house looked both elegant and welcoming; the table, dazzling with candle-lit silver and crystal. Dinner was delicious, surpassing even their high expectations, and Maggie defiantly accepted a second slice of the amazing mocha-hazelnut torte. After all, it was her birthday cake, her night. As soon as dessert was finished, Young Frank whisked Rob off to computerland and the adults drifted over to the living room for coffee.

"That was a wonderful dinner, and a beautiful table," Maggie told her sister-in-law. "You are amazing. You really are the superwoman we all aspired to be. Right, Barbie?" Cecile fussed with the sugar tongs, blushing.

Dave tactlessly asked, "Where is Karyn? Not ill, I hope."

Since the parents had not mentioned it, Maggie and Barbara had skirted the subject of Karyn's absence all evening; Alexis pretended not to notice. Later, she admitted in confidence that she figured the girl had blown off her aunt's birthday party in favour of some rock concert or teenybopper dance. Maggie had a similar suspicion and was slightly hurt.

"Not ill," Stan muttered, "just mad."

"Which kind of mad," Dave the bloodhound persisted, "angry or crazy?"

"How do you tell, with a teenager? Sulking," was all the information Stan was willing to impart. His father volunteered cryptically: "Confined to barracks, until further notice. An exception was made for tonight, but she's boycotting, 'cause the furlough was contingent on a dress-code. No décolletage."

Maggie stared at Cecile, the supermom. "What on earth...?"

"Oh, all right. The silly girl went and had herself tattooed – after we expressly forbade it." Her face began to crumple, as close to tears as Maggie had ever seen her. "She's only thirteen! Disfigured for life!"

Knowing better than to butt in when other parents had a problem with their child, both Dave and Maggie dropped the subject. They discussed a range of other topics until it was time to collect their own offspring and say goodnight. In the car

Rob was so fidgety with suppressed mirth that his father finally demanded: "Spill, comrade!"

Rob laughed out loud. "I saw it. Kary's tattoo. I don't know what her mom's so freaked out over. It's just flowers and stuff. Like, a necklace of roses and stuff – kind of pretty."

Maggie asked, "What does 'and stuff' entail, exactly?"

"Well, um, like, geckos and skinks. Pretty cool."

Maggie and Dave spoke with emphasis, in unison. "Don't even think it!"

And said no more all the way home, lest their own suppressed juvenile sentiments undermine their adult authority. The parents dared not exchange so much as a surreptitious glance, but her hand, of its own volition, crept across the seat to rest on his thigh and they could both feel the boy behind them grinning. For a moment they were, all three, in tune.

Maggie had not felt up to yet another party with the same old crowd, but Barb wanted her meet the latest boyfriend. He turned out much as expected: a big friendly jock with no intellectual pretensions. Maggie wandered from group to group, listening to snatches of conversation, none of which she was tempted to join. She busied herself picking chips off the floor, emptying ashtrays and collecting glasses for an excuse at escapes to the kitchen. The music was too loud and people would periodically disappear into the bedroom, singly or in pairs, to re-emerge with little purple eyes, giggling uncontrollably.

Popular Lix had already chosen a partner for the night; her rejects were desultorily casing the room for available females. John-the-Freak occupied himself devouring every scrap of food in the apartment. A group centered on Revolting John vehemently debated the strategy of power politics. Dennis had brought along an unfamiliar friend, and Maggie watched him curiously. Though not her type, there was something oddly attractive about this fair boy with too much curly hair.

John was saying, "You college boys, with your neat little jackets and neat little ties and neat little plans," he fixed Dennis, in jeans and a sweatshirt, with blazing, red-rimmed eyes. "What good are you to the movement?" Dennis turned away without bothering to answer, so John rounded on his companion: "What are you gonna do when all the shit goes down?"

"I don't know," the boy answered. "It depends."

Tessa, who had a weakness for skinny blonds, turned to him teasingly, "He's not a revolutionary, are you, Davey?"

"Probably not," he replied in a serious tone, never breaking eye-contact with John. "I'm slow. A plodder, not a firebrand. Revolutions happen too fast."

"So, what are you gonna do?" John persisted.

The boy called Davey shrugged. "I guess, maybe follow you around, trying to repair the good things you break."

Maggie waited until the confrontation passed, conversations resumed and everyone's attention moved elsewhere, then caught his eye and smiled.

He smiled back and came over. They went for a walk in the cool night.

She slipped out of bed and down the stairs, quietly, barefoot. With no particular objective in mind, but restless, she fetched a glass of milk and sat in the den. An old B&W costume drama on the late show provided undemanding company. Maggie pondered her family, her marriage, her thirty-eighth year.

How can something so good feel so wrong? When you have everything you ever wanted, why are you still dissatisfied? How does the worked-for, saved-for dream house turn into a warehouse for things? How does the longed-for, perfect child become a source of endless frustration? Where does all the potential go?

How they had planned it was that Maggie would work until they could afford a solid home in a clean, safe environment in which to bring up Robbie and his little sister – hopefully; a little brother would be fine too. Once Dave was established as an independent contractor, she would turn her attention to family and to developing her musical talent. But the second child never came, never could, and she subsumed her loss in a career. The good second-hand Steinway Dave had given her eight birthdays ago sat in a corner of the unused dining room; she'd never had time to master it beyond the level of entertaining at Christmas. Though they owned a spacious corner lot, nobody had the energy to do more than mow the lawn, nor sit out and enjoy even that. Why?

Dave slid onto the end of the couch. "I'm not here to disturb you," he whispered.

"It's okay," she replied, "I've seen this before." In truth, she could not even recall what film she was ignoring.

"Oh, yes, one of my favourites. I used to think how wonderful, how heroic it was to renounce everything, even life itself, for the loved one. I used to identify with Sidney Carton." He sighed. "Now, I'm not sure. The older I grow, the more attached I grow. I hate to give anything up. I want to find ways to eat my cake and have it, too." He paused to take a sip of milk; Maggie waited. "Still," he concluded after a short silence, "if I had to, I could probably sort out what's important, and let the rest go."

Maggie stared at her husband under cover of a gloomy scene. What was this about?

"Sorry," Dave said. "You were thinking and I was intruding. " He padded off as softly as he'd come.

Hate to give up anything... Yes, she did. And yet, if happiness is value, much of what she had was without value. In youth, she had never been afraid to let go, to make a change, nor to move on, never looking back in regret.

She had her backpack, containing only such things as she owned outright, and her guitar. She knew her destination. Classmates Barb and Lix had just rented a flat in Toronto; they would let her crash for a while. She had skills and good references from summer jobs and could count on being able to contribute very soon. Determined to take nothing from her parents, the tricky part would be earning enough to live on, since the scholarship covered tuition only. There was a whole summer ahead to work out the details.

Mrs. Simpson was in tears, of course. Since crying was her fall-back strategy in any conflict of interest, the girls had ceased to pay attention years ago. The tears would dry up, once she realized that Margaret gone was a Margaret who created no problems, started no arguments, expressed no embarrassing opinions, made no waves. Besides, she would have Gwendolyn's wedding to keep her fully occupied – deciding which of her social contacts, which of Father's clients and associates, would be most advantageous to invite; trying to determine which colour scheme was most in vogue in New York and Paris – and would the people she hoped to impress know the difference?

Poor Gwen! Maybe… Then again, it was so hard to tell. Gwen seemed comfortable enough letting Mother organize her, dress her, manage her; it was easier than growing a mind of her own. Soon she would be married and away; make an excellent wife for an up-and-coming young Tory like

Anthony Collins. Tony the Tory… Gwen may well have internalized the art of manipulation; may well be on her way to becoming her Mother. In a year or two, the sisters would have nothing in common.

But Margaret promised herself to keep in touch with Father. Poor him, too. He might be a big wheel at Graydon, Upshaw and Simpson; at home he did whatever stopped the tears. Joined the right clubs, attended the right fund-raising balls. What did he really think? What did he really want? Besides making his wife happy, that is, which was impossible.

They had moved four times in twelve years – to finer houses at better addresses – transferring their daughters to a more expensive, exclusive and repressive private school. Margaret was always an A student but the uniforms and deportment rules and snobbery had been increasingly irksome. Only because she was determined to get a degree had she hung on to the very last, graduating with a 94% average. Never a popular girl, her only two friends were already gone.

There was nothing left here. She would make her own way, decide her own course, set her own priorities. Marry? Maybe, someday, if she found the right man. It must be possible to establish balance in a relationship, where nobody is used and nobody is dragged along behind the other's will. She would settle for nothing less than an equal partnership. Margaret Edwina Simpson would not settle for less. In the meantime, she could take care of herself.

Was I really that judgmental, that arrogant? Oh yes. Isn't everyone, at eighteen? The real question is: have I grown any more tolerant, any wiser, in twenty years? Am I what I intended to be? Have I done what I meant to do? We *are* a good team. Davey keeps the faith; Maggie keeps the books – that was the contract. The important things are as solid as ever. We *have* arrived where we wanted to be. Where do we go from here?

Sunday dawned as bright and clear as any Christmas card. Maggie, who had slept less than three hours, felt bright and clear, too, strangely enough. She hummed a little half-forgotten tune while preparing breakfast. That was usually Dave's job on a Sunday.

He eyed the twin boiled eggs and slices of toast with misgiving. "I don't mind frying some bacon - honestly."

"That's sufficient for a man on a diet," Maggie declared.

"Who says I'm on a diet? Since when?"

"I do. Since I saw your brother last night."

"Oh, Okay," he said, holding up a slice of toast by its corner, "but I do I at least get to put jam on this?"

"Sure, and honey or peanut butter on the other one, if you like. I mean to keep you gorgeous, not starve you to death. Then, before Rob wakes up, we could maybe take a walk in the snow. All right?"

"All right!" Dave brightened instantly. "We haven't done that in ages."

"I've been thinking," Maggie said, "and I'd like to discuss some things."

"Shoot," he said, "I'm all ears." Dave paid attention, as he always did, seriously. Even the toast lay neglected on his plate.

"First, we need to lighten up. Cut Robbie a little more slack, have a little more fun, say what we really feel a little more often, even if it's undiplomatic. Stop trying to be perfect. We're okay, but we could be happier."

"Works for me!"

"Second, about our vacation. What if we went in spring break? It's only a week, I know, but this may be the last year Rob goes anywhere with us, and I don't want to miss the chance. Let's ask him what he'd like to do. But," she cautioned as Dave began to nod in energetic agreement, "we can't be too extravagant."

"I thought we were pretty flush."

"We are. Only…. That's the third thing. What if I quit?"

His mouth fell open for a fraction a second. He slammed it shut on a muffled "What?"

"I mean, quit work. Stay home. Plant a vegetable garden. Bake muffins. Balance your ledgers and do a little freelancing. Practice piano. I have… Promise not to laugh! I have this weird notion of setting tax forms to music."

 He spread jam around on his toast and then spread it again in the opposite direction, staring fixedly at it the whole time. Whatever his down-turned face was doing, she heard not the slightest hint of a giggle. See, she thought, I did find the right man.

Dave looked up at his wife. "Lady, when you do some thinking, you do *not* mess around! We have some *major* planning to do. Not to mention house renovation. You'll need a sound studio."

"Of course, I can't let the firm down, have to stay
till crazy season is over, May or June. Then I'd like
another vacation. Maybe we could drive out to the
coast – without Rob?"

Time Scope

by Francis Mont

Zack Dougall stared at the gizmo on the garage sale bench. It looked weird. A plywood box of about 2 feet cube, with an old fashioned CRT screen at the front, and a row of control buttons under it. The back was open, revealing an interior jammed full of electronic circuit boards and a wire-mesh of a peculiar pattern attached to two walls and to the top.

"What the heck is that?" he asked the old man sitting in his garden chair behind the bench.

"I wish I knew. It's from the estate of my late tenant who used to live there." He poked his thumb in the direction of a small clapboard building in the back of his property.

"So what happened to him?" Zack was curious. Taking a closer look at the device, he saw seven controls, labelled 'Power', 'Time', 'Space', 'Zoom', 'Speed', 'Scan' and 'Track'. Some were pushbuttons, some rotary dials. He also found four small buttons with arrows pointing left, right, up and down. He expected volume control and channel selection but found none.

"He passed away, last month. Brain cancer." The landlord sighed, shaking his head sadly. "Was still very young, no more than twenty-six, twenty-eight. People shouldn't die that early."

"So what do you think this thing is?" Zack prompted. "Did he ever tell you about it?"

"Oh he talked about it all the time. The big invention that was going to make him rich"

"What's it supposed to do?"

"That, he never said. He was very secretive about it but kept telling me to be patient with the rent because once he sold it, he'd pay me tenfold."

"And you believed him?"

"I was sorry for him. You see, he was invalided out of the engineering corps, got wounded in Iraq and retired on a VA pension. I'm a vet myself, seen quite a bit of action and I know how hard it can get. I cut him a lot of slack."

"So he was an engineer?"

"They trained him in electronics when he joined up, after he dropped out of the MIT Physics program. Thought he was too smart for them".

"Did he leave anything besides this gadget? Notes, diagrams - some clue as to what this is supposed to be?"

"There is a box full of crap like that left in his workshop, nothing valuable any more. Those I already sold."

"Such as?"

"An oscilloscope, instruments of all kinds. Most of them I couldn't name, but someone picked them all up. The rest is just junk. I was planning to take it to the dump today, after I closed down here."

"Do you mind if I have a look?" Zack asked eagerly.

"Be my guest, but don't take too long."

"Thanks. Please don't sell this to anyone until I come back. I might buy it myself."

As the old veteran said, the house and the workshop were empty, except for a big cardboard box on a workbench. It contained all kinds of things thrown in randomly. Components, circuit boards, cables, metal brackets, soldering kit and many sheets of paper with hand-drawn circuit diagrams, lots of notes and a badly stained and scribbled-over manuscript.

He picked it up and looked at the title. "E for Effort" by T. L. Sherred.

It was a stapled photocopy of a science fiction story Zack had read as a child. He gasped, because now he knew what the inventor had been attempting to accomplish. He wasted no time returning to the front yard.

"How much do you want for it?" he asked, out of breath.

"I don't know. Make me an offer?"

"I'll give you fifty bucks." Zack hoped he had picked the right amount, not too high to make him suspicious, not too low to be rejected.

The old man chuckled. "You must be some kind of nut. You can have it".

Zack handed over the cash and, with some help, loaded the device in the back of his van.

"Do you mind if I take that junk too?

"Not at all, son, saves me a trip!"

The old man watched with amusement as Zack staggered from the workshop to his car under the weight of the box.

"Now, drive safely!" He laughed out loud, shaking his head as Zack drove away.

~

Zack had a long drive home from Farmington, Connecticut where he found his prize - yet one more funky electronic device acquired on his latest cross-country hunting trip. Not that he needed any more. His house in DC, his basement, even his garage were chock full of quaint gadgets and contraptions – some of them clean and labelled, some still dusty and unidentified, just as he'd found them at one garage sale or another. Zack's hobby was collecting 'antique' technology. He was a passionate tinkerer and prided himself on making old machines work.

He did not dare to think that this one could function. His driving became a bit erratic as he kept twisting his neck to look back at the big box winking at him with its lifeless screen.

That was science fiction and this is real life. Stop your silly dreams and focus on driving, before you end up in a ditch! Now all the controls make sense. That man was trying to build a 'Time Scope', a device that could be tuned to any space and time coordinate and observe the events as they actually took place.

The background of the inventor sounded right: Physics at MIT, electronic engineering training at the army, he had the prerequisites. But to build a time machine, even if only a limited viewing device, seemed too fantastic. Zack could hardly wait to get home and try it out.

On second thought, he couldn't. He pulled into a McDonald's parking lot and collected the sheets of paper, notes and diagrams from the jumble of small tools and components in the cardboard box. When he had them all, he went in for a coffee, taking the papers with him.

Some of the notes were test results, all suggesting success. Others were specifications on the power supply he would need. Several sheets were covered with tightly written differential equations. He recognized Einstein's space-time diagram, transformation formulas for momentum-energy and electric and magnetic fields. The Lorentz Transformation Formulas were prominent on every page. Some were plans on marketing it to the highest bidder, once the final touches were complete.

Zack could hardly breathe, wiping sweat off his forehead.

Holy crap, this might be actually happening!

~

Tired by the time he got home, he forced himself to put off further investigation until the following day. He woke just after dawn, and spent hours patiently wiring together power supplies and transformers, then testing and starting over, to find the right combination. He also needed to hook up an oscilloscope and a digital signal generator for calibration. Without the wiring diagrams in the notes, it would have been impossible to figure out.

When Zack finally turned it on, little dials over some of the controls were illuminated, as if waiting for him to input a desired setting. He decided not to change the time and space dials for the first try and pushed the 'Scan' knob.

The picture-tube came alive, focused and, after a few minutes, started showing a silent movie. A huge, badly-dressed crowd in a wide public square, waving flags and placards Zack couldn't read faced a podium with a skinny bearded man on it, moving his mouth and gesticulating. Using the 'Zoom' knob, he identified the speaker as Vladimir Lenin. The 'Time' dial showed September 3, 1917.

He needed another confirmation. Quickly.

He set the 'Space' dial to New York and the 'Time' dial to September 11, 2001. He finessed it forward to morning. It showed the World Trade Center standing tall and proud on a clear bright September morning. And then came a low-flying jumbo jet and Zack watched in horror as it plunged into the wall and burst into flames. Fifteen *actual* minutes later, he could track the second plane careening toward and striking the south tower, all in eerie silence.

One more try before he dared allow himself to be convinced.

For the 'Space' setting he looked up the GPS coordinates of his own address. For 'Time' he picked Aug 28 of last year, two days before he had sold his used Hyundai. Then pressed the 'Scan' button. On the TV screen his house and driveway appeared, with himself out front, taking an hour to wash and wax the car.

He could not have any more doubt. He had acquired a goddamn, functional time machine.

Further testing familiarized him with all the controls on the device. What he liked most was the 'Track' option that enabled him to focus on one person, animal, or vehicle via the 'Zoom' feature and then, by pushing the 'Track' control knob, have the 'Time Scope' automatically adjust the space and time coordinates, so he could follow the movement of the selected subject wherever it went. He could even speed up, or slow down, the tracking by the 'Speed" rotary control. The man who invented this was a genius, no doubt about that!

Why, I can spy on anyone, anywhere, any time – maybe even look into the future and learn the lottery numbers for the next draw or pick a high yielding stock and get as rich as I want.

This second idea, however, did not seem possible. No time coordinate beyond the current date was available.

~

His ruminations were interrupted by the doorbell. *This must be Suzy, she had said she would drop by this afternoon.*

Zack quickly covered his gadget with a plastic sheet, and left his workshop, closing the door behind him. He wasn't ready to discuss this unexpected event with anyone – least of all Susan. He knew how impulsive she was and how aggressive she could be. Until he decided how to handle it, he wanted to keep it secret.

He opened the door and felt the usual dizziness on seeing her face and gorgeous body – he could never have enough of either. She wore cutoff jeans and a low cut tank top, her blond hair swirling freely around her face. But that face was serious now, not her usual impish smile.

"Zack," she demanded, "have you shaved yet today? Look at you - you look like a bum!"

Zack inspected his reflection in the hall mirror and saw nothing wrong. He was tall and lanky, with a narrow face and a shock of black, curly hair that seemed to defy all attempts to be kept in some recognizable shape. The worn-out work clothes he usually had on in his lab did not improve the image.

That's the way I always look, so what's her problem?

"We need to talk," she declared, giving him pause: he wasn't used to her stern voice. "I am not crazy about the way things are going between us." she blurted out. Zack started to protest but she silenced him with a gesture. "Let me finish. You have been out of a job for over a year, you are cooped up here, playing with your weird toys, living on god only knows what…"

Her boyfriend tried to stop the tirade, but she wouldn't be stopped. Not this time. "…and you are dragging me down with you. Our relationship is going nowhere and I am tired of this stagnation."

"But Suzy…" he tried, and got slapped down again.

"Zack, this is an ultimatum. Unless you start behaving like a regular guy with a regular job, we are finished. Go out and find some work. Call me when you have."

With this last demand, she turned and flounced out of his house. Zack was stunned. He had not expected this.

Two things were unthinkable in his universe: life without Suzy and a regular job. So far, he had managed to survive on his fast dwindling inheritance, and he knew it wouldn't last much longer. His tinkering hobby was eating up way more than he admitted to himself and he knew he had to do something to get hold of more funds if he meant to keep both his girl and his hobby. He wasn't quite sure in what order.

He shuffled slowly back to his lab and absent-mindedly pulled the sheet off the 'Time Scope'.

The germ of an idea began forming in his mind. *What if I could use it to lay my hands on some serious money?*

He knew that spying on the future was out. What if he spied on the past? How could he make money with that? Blackmail was an obvious possibility but he knew he would never sink that low. What else could he do?

He remembered a newspaper article that suggested a connection between Senator Hopkins and the infamous Mafia boss, Joe Petuccini – an allegation that the senator vehemently denied. The headline was: "Senator Hopkins meets with Joe Petuccini – questions asked".

The paper referred to 'sources' claiming that the senator interfered with a criminal police investigation, concerning one of Petuccini's associates, and raised the question of influence-peddling. An appointment in the senator's office, on September 14th, was on record. The article speculated on subsequent meetings, but admittedly had no evidence of any. The paper showed their two photos, side by side, which was a nasty insinuation by itself, Zack thought.

Zack didn't believe a word of it. He respected Senator Hopkins, knew him to be an honourable man and rolled his eyes at how the muckraking media were going after Hopkins. *They like to stir up shit about anyone if it helps them sell papers!*

Maybe I could use this device to prove them wrong?

Zack realized all he needed to do was tune his 'Time Scope' to the senator's office, and use the 'Track' option to follow him around. He did not need to track continuously, but could skip ahead as the situation allowed. He would find out if there was a second, more clandestine meeting between the two. If there was, he could see for himself, and maybe show the world what really happened?

Hey, I should set up as a detective agency and use the device to solve crimes. I bet there is substantial reward for some of these cold cases and it might be a steady income from an unsteady job I could do at home! So, this project would also be a good exercise in learning to use the machine!

~

It was the most boring week of his life, glued to his 'Time Scope', tuned to 5:00PM every day of the past two weeks when the senator left his office. Zack quickly zoomed in on him and then pushed the 'Track' button. The 'Time Scope' worked like a charm. He leaned back in his chair and watched the senator going about his daily routine, all the way through town, stopping here and there, meeting with people, none of whom` was Petuccini.

Zack spent maddeningly slow days watching Hopkins arrive home, eat his dinner, read a book, sip his tea, light his pipe, scratch his neck and do other totally mundane things.

Won't he do anything interesting for a change?

He almost gave up the idea when, on the fifth day of his vigil, he saw the senator walk outside and get into his car. The 'Time Scope' followed him along M Street to Georgetown Mall. He drove down the ramp to the underground garage. When he got out, a dark blue Caddy that had followed him pulled up alongside and stopped. A burly figure emerged from the backseat and walked up to the senator – Zack couldn't believe it – he saw Joe Petuccini's familiar face.

Holy crap! They did actually meet, and in an underground garage, late at night! I wouldn't have expected this! Quickly picking up his cell phone, he focused on the screen, and started filming. He had no idea what they talked about, but whatever it was, it didn't last long. The senator shook his head and abruptly walked away toward the elevator. Zack copied down the date and time: September 26, 8:36PM.

This looked like an encounter unexpected by Senator Hopkins and could prove his innocence. Zack already had the senator's email address and now he sent a very short message with the video clip attached.

He'll find it tomorrow and I'll be ready for his call.

~

Senator Hopkins enjoyed a quiet afternoon in his office, spent mostly on opening mail, both e and otherwise, from his constituents. He liked to deal with ordinary folks' problems, questions and requests. It made him feel that he was doing something useful, away from the frustrating political infighting that came with his job.

But now he was confused. The email he'd just opened contained a video clip of him and Joe Petuccini, in the parking garage. The text only said: "we need to talk" and a phone number. The clip was legitimate, showing a scene that had really taken place. If this became public, he could be ruined. Nobody would believe how innocent he was.

Gordon Hopkins was a rarity, an endangered species in Washington: an honest, principled and, most of all, incorruptible politician. In a career of almost thirty-seven years he had avoided temptations, scandals, even the slightest suggestion of impropriety, until recently, when those speculations started about him and Petuccini.

They had first met when the casino tycoon came to his office, asking Hopkins to intercede on behalf of one of his 'associates'. The man, according to

Petuccini, was wrongfully arrested, presumably to put pressure on himself. Hopkins served on the senate judiciary committee, so Petuccini assumed that he had influence. The senator briefly looked into the case, decided that he had no jurisdiction and forgot about it.

Shortly after that, the rumours started. Senator Hopkins had a pretty good idea who had started them. His unscrupulous rival, Jack Cringe, must have heard about the case and wasted no time in using the appearance of collusion against him.

Then, a week ago, when he had driven to his usual shopping mall for groceries, he was accosted by the alleged gangster in the parking garage. He told Petuccini that he could do nothing to help him and walked away.

And now this!

Who on earth could have taken that clear, sharp clip in the under-illuminated garage? He had to find out. Reluctantly, he dialed the number. After making sure that the person who answered was the originator of the email, he said: "You have a 3:00 PM appointment in my office this afternoon," and hung up.

Zack was shocked by the summons. *Maybe he thinks I'm trying to blackmail him?*

He knew the senator would demand to know how he had acquired the video and he wasn't prepared

to reveal that. *They'll take the 'Time Scope' away!
It's mine and I want to keep it. My future
professional income, never mind my love life, may
depend on it.*

He decided to say that he had been sitting in his
car, waiting for a friend, when he'd seen the
senator and Petuccini together and, on an
impulse, he shot the video for his celebrity
collection. With this cover story ready in his head,
and not a little apprehension, he drove to the
Senate building.

Hopkins was all smiles; he invited Zack to sit on
the padded leather chair across from his desk,
then asked point blank: "Mr. Dougall, I need to
know how you acquired the video clip you sent
me."

Oh my God, Zack groaned inwardly, *he already
knows my name.*

He quickly rattled off his prepared speech and,
strangely, the senator seemed to accept it.

"Well, then," Hopkins said, "what do you intend to
do with this?"

"Senator", Zack blurted out, surprising even
himself, "I've been thinking of starting my own
detective agency, so I set out to prove your
innocence. Partly because I'm certain you are,

partly because I hope to use your reference in advertising."

"Zack... may I call you Zack?"

"Oh, sure, if you like," Zack stammered.

"Zack, that was very noble of you, wanting to help clear my name and I am sure I wouldn't mind returning the favour in the future, but first I must deal with my own problem. Let me ask you: were you there all the time that Petuccini and I were together? How long would you say that event lasted?"

"Not more than a minute, senator"

"And, during that minute, did you see anything inappropriate? Did anything pass between us? Any document? Any object?"

"Oh, God, no sir, nothing like that, I 'm quite sure. I had a clear view and you were not standing close enough to hand over anything".

Zack relaxed. The senator did not seem to be after his hide; rather, trying to save his own.

"Look here son", Hopkins continued, "there are these nasty rumours going around about me, and I know who started them but, until now, I had no way to counter them."

He smiled at Zack reassuringly: "However, now I have a witness to the only other brief meeting, if you can call it that, I had with that man. So what I suggest: *We* call a press conference and present your video clip, and your story, to the reporters. That way we nip any further rumours in the bud."

Zack wanted to protest, but the senator held up his hand: "I am sorry, but your participation is necessary and you won't get into trouble, I promise. After that, you may use my name as reference for your business. This is my price."

~

Joe Petuccini watched the press conference on TV and was not amused. Senator Hopkins told the assembled reporters about the video clip in his possession, explained how he had acquired it and briefly showed it on his tablet computer. He also introduced the witness who gave him the video and could be called to testify if the need arose.

Petuccini was perplexed. He wasn't sure what he should do. Could that video get him into trouble? What else did the senator have on him? What else did the photographer snap pictures of?

~

Zack saw the news item as well and was not at all pleased. He suddenly found himself in a dubious position, expecting the press at his door any minute. It turned out it wasn't reporters he needed to worry about.

The knock came late at night. Opening the door, he found himself face to face with Joe Petuccini, the infamous crime boss, and two tall, muscular men standing behind him.

"Hello," Zack said in a shaky voice, "can I help you?"

Petuccini smiled.

"I sure hope you can," he said sweetly, "for your own sake. May we come in?"

Chapter 2

Senator Hopkins arrived an hour later.

He had never meant to visit Zack, but something in the back of his mind just wouldn't stop nagging, until he took another look at that video clip. The more times he watched, the more convinced he became that Zack's story of shooting that video from his car was untrue.

It took him a while to realize that the angle was wrong. The image was taken from considerably higher than where a person, sitting in his car – any car – would be positioned. Actually, not even a tall person, standing up, could have achieved that angle. *What was Zack hiding? How did he really acquire that footage? He must have gotten hold of a security camera tape, but how?* Hopkins had to find out.

When the doorbell rang again, Zack jumped up to answer, but Petuccini waved him back to the couch and signaled one of his shadows to see who it was. He recognized the voice immediately from the hallway and called out in the voice of a jovial host.

"Come on in, senator, the more the merrier!"

Gordon Hopkins stopped inside the living room door to take in the scene.

Zack was huddled in the corner of a sofa, obviously scared, but unharmed, so far. Petuccini was lounging comfortably in one of the armchairs, with a quizzical look on his face. Two expressionless bodyguards stood behind him.

Petuccini was the first to speak. "Looks like we are both after the same thing. I bet you came to discover how this gentleman acquired the video clip you showed the journalists. I must admit a similar curiosity prompted me, as well."

Hopkins considered this friendly opening and decided to play along for the time being. "I see you've made yourself at home. Have you come to any conclusion as to how it was possible? Did this *gentleman* divulge his secret? He seems to be still in one piece."

"Oh, he was very cooperative," Petuccini said with a barely suppressed smile, "once he saw the alternative to cooperation. Only," he added, "I am not sure that I believe his story."

They all focused on Zack, who so far had not uttered a word. During this exchange, however, he seemed to relax a little and his birdlike features took on thoughtful aspect. He turned to the senator, as if for support, and said, "I have a very valuable secret, sir. Actually, it can be extremely valuable to both of you, but only until anyone else finds out." He looked pointedly at Petuccini's silent companions.

Petuccini was intrigued, considered the implications, and then nodded toward the exit. His bodyguards quietly opened the front door and went outside.

"Happy? We are alone and all ears – and you still have yours. Make your pitch."

"I'd better show you, or you wouldn't believe me," said Zack and, confidently for the first time that night, stood up and led them to the other room.

It needed a minute for the other two to take in the electronic workshop, with built-in benches around the walls, a large table in the centre, and a jungle of wires and cables connecting odd contraptions that surrounded what looked like a home-made television on the central table.

Zack pointed to the TV. "What would you say if I told you that with this set I can spy on anyone, anywhere, any time in the past?"

The senator rolled his eyes.

Petuccini caressed his right earlobe. "I would say: prove that assertion, or you will regret wasting my time."

"Very well," Senator Hopkins challenged, "I always wanted to know whether Oswald was really at the window when Kennedy was shot. If you can show us that scene, I will believe you, however fantastic this claim sounds."

Zack spent a few minutes acquiring the space and time coordinates from the internet and then started fiddling with the knobs and dials on his outlandish device.

His two 'guests' were mesmerized, watching him fine tune his contraption as he zoomed in on the sixth floor of the Dallas school book depository.

Nothing happened for a while, but then they saw a window slowly open and the barrel of a rifle protrude through the crack, with a shadow holding it, barely visible inside the dark room. They couldn't identify the man on the view-screen, but clearly saw flames erupt from the rifle. Since the 'Time Scope' did not provide sound, the effect of these silent shots was all the more dramatic.

Zack looked up from his seat at his stunned visitors.

The senator sat down heavily on the only other chair in the room, while Petuccini emitted a low whistle, rubbing his temples with both hands.

Minutes passed before anyone spoke again.

Finally, Petuccini said, his voice a bit shaky: "Gentlemen, it appears we have both an opportunity and a problem."

"Yes. Oh, yes," Hopkins croaked. Clearing his throat, said, "This thing," he pointed at the TV with a not too steady finger, "could be extremely dangerous in the wrong hands."

"To whose hands are you referring, senator?" asked Petuccini softly, raising an eyebrow. "I believe we must come to some kind of agreement here. Obviously, only the three of us can know about this."

"Three?" asked the senator, looking at Zack who was struggling with conflicting emotions. His fear was gradually giving way to resolve.

He said, somewhat petulantly: "There is no way either of you could operate this device without me. It's built into my lab that provides the very delicately calibrated power it needs." To drive home this point, he added, "And you need me to control it, because it's awfully hard to tune correctly. So, whatever agreement you make, count me in."

Petuccini looked at the jumble of wires and nodded. "He may be right about that, senator. It seems we do need the young maestro to play this instrument." After a thoughtful pause he added, "And, I am sure, you wouldn't dream of cutting *me* out, because you know that if either of us mentions our secret outside this room, we both lose our chances forever." He chuckled without genuine amusement. "It wouldn't take long for the FBI, CIA, NSA and all the rest of the alphabet to swoop down and make it disappear. Maybe us, too."

Senator Hopkins considered. Finally, he said: "I'm willing to agree on one condition. That neither of us be allowed to use it for any purpose whatsoever that the other objects to." Petuccini tried to interrupt, but Hopkins raised a peremptory hand. "If Zack can set it up in such a way that operating it required us each to enter an encrypted password, then we both would have to be present, before it could be turned on."

Zack, for the first time since the senator had arrived, exclaimed confidently. "Sure! I can hook up the power supply through the computer and hardwire a relay switch directly into a programmable circuit board to close the switch only when passwords are recognized." He said it, eagerly – maybe a bit too eagerly.

"Yes, I am sure you could," remarked Petuccini, "but what would prevent *you* from using it any time you want to, for god only knows what nefarious purpose, like what you tried to pull on the senator here?"

"I didn't pull anything! I was only trying to help him clear his name!" Zack almost shouted, then added more calmly "I guess you'll have to trust me…" but stopped when he saw the gangster's face.

"I guess we won't," said Petuccini, in a very firm tone. "Instead," he continued more softly, "I'll arrange my own kind of security. I will have a lock installed on this room, so that you can't get in unless I open it." Zack, who started to protest, was silenced with a glance. "Make sure you remove everything from here that you can't live without, except whatever this… machine needs. One of my serviceman will call on you tomorrow morning to do the work."

Zack knew when to shut up. He didn't have a choice.

The senator, however, wasn't satisfied yet.

"I know what I want to use it for, and we can discuss it later, but I must tell you, Mr. Petuccini, that I won't agree to anything criminal. If you wish to do research that does not involve anything illegal, we can have a deal."

Surprisingly, he met no argument.

"I knew it had to be something like that. I have a few personal questions, particularly as regards the comings and goings, during the last few weeks, of my less than trustworthy mistress."

Hopkins could not suppress a smile at that revelation – the feared gangster was jealous!

Petuccini added, "If you can go along with that, and I promise no physical harm comes to her even if I find my suspicions confirmed, then, yes, we have a deal."

Senator Hopkins considered this an acceptable price for the information he so desperately desired, concerning his own party's presidential nominee. Hopkins suspected a dark, hidden agenda behind that man and he needed to know whether his election would lurch the country onto a dangerous course.

Finally, he said: "Agreed. Now we only need to determine which of us will use the machine first. As I don't think it would be a good idea to run simultaneous research projects, I propose to do one at a time. Shall we flip a coin to decide?"

Petuccini immediately pulled a silver dollar from his pocket, ready to toss but the senator stayed his hand: "Zack, do you have any change?"

Zack produced a quarter and tossed it. Petuccini won. They agreed on a day, after the locks were installed and Zack had done the computer hookup, to meet again.

Joe Petuccini, driven off in his limo, wondered whether he really wanted to know the truth about Maria. *So what if she is having some fun on the side?* The trouble was, he liked her too much. Depended on her too much. N*eeded* to know how far he could trust her.

~

Senator Hopkins was deep in thought on his way home. He knew that he had an opportunity, a terrifyingly dangerous one, to make a decisive difference, for first time in his political career. An opportunity to save his country from a frightening change of direction. He had been unhappy with the way things were going. If he were to make a list of all the things wrong with his country, it would be a very long one.

On top of this list was this anger and resentment that seemed to permeate the news he read, the interviews he heard, the daily rallies and demonstrations against another incident of police brutality, the seemingly random mass shootings. The mood of the country was ugly: people were fed up and wanted change. *Any* change. That was the big problem. When there is a wave, you will always find those who ride it to personal success, regardless of consequences.

It was happening all over the world, unscrupulous politicians and rabble rousing demagogues were popping up everywhere, fueling fear, hatred, suspicion – setting themselves up as the only ones who could save the frightened and angry population. The news of the world disturbed him, but Hopkins was primarily concerned with his own country, and within that, in particular, with his own party, and its new leader.

Though he had some preliminary reading to do, by the time he got home, Hopkins was determined to follow through with this crazy scheme. But first, he needed to discuss this with Muriel. She was his oldest friend and confidant. If anyone could give him sound advice, she was the one.

They had been married back when they were both too young to know what they wanted to do with their lives. It had taken fifteen years to figure it out that their career paths required different settings: his in Washington, hers in Vermont. He had become a politician; she, an artist. The divorce had been amicable; they had no dispute over property and no children.

They reconnected from time to time, when either needed a trusted friend to help to work through a difficult problem or dilemma, and Hopkins realized that now it was his moment to call her.

~

When the phone rang, Muriel was busy carving the cedar log she had salvaged from her woods that morning. *Let it ring*, she thought. *Can't be important!* Then she heard Gordon's voice leaving a message. She dropped her mallet and chisel and scrambled to get to the phone before he could hang up.

"Gordon," she gasped, out of breath from running across two rooms, "what kind of trouble are you in now?"

Hopkins chuckled. "I love you too, Muriel, how have you been?"

"I guess I must do," she admitted grudgingly, unable to stop a furtive glance in the wall mirror over the hall table, unaware that her hand flew to her hair in a vain attempt to smooth down her cowlicks.

"I've been fine. Busy as usual. I just managed to drag home a beautiful cedar log thick enough to carve that turtle I'd been planning."

Hearing Gordon's suppressed laugh, she added hastily: "…but I guess you didn't call me about turtles."

Hopkins appreciated her quick understanding. "No, Muriel. I need to talk to you about something very important that just came up."

It was Muriel's turn to chuckle. "Tell me one thing in your life that's *not* very important! Well, what's today's earth shaking emergency?"

"Not over the phone, Muriel. We have to meet, and the sooner the better. If it's all right with you, I'll catch the evening commuter flight and be there in a few hours."

Muriel was flabbergasted. "Then it must really be important. If you give me the flight number and arrival time, I'll pick you up".

After he rang off, she reflected on how strange their relationship had grown over the decades. She had to admit to herself that Gordon was the only human being she trusted implicitly. She respected his integrity and dedication to doing as much good as he could.

It must be a serious crisis, for him to drop everything and fly up here, at a moment's notice, just to consult his old friend.

Gordon Hopkins' heart missed a beat when he caught sight of Muriel at 'Arrivals'. She was tall and erect, her pure white hair tied in a girlish ponytail. Under the inevitable layers of years, the oh-so-familiar face was as lovely as he remembered it from college.

After they hugged, they walked in silence to her car, then navigated slowly out of Montpelier

International Airport. Muriel lived only an hour's drive outside the city, in a log house on a hundred wooded acres.

They didn't talk about his mission until they were comfortably seated in her living room, looking at the dark trees outside the floor- to- ceiling windows that covered one entire wall.

"Okay, Gordon, tell me," she opened the serious discussion.

"What would you say, Muriel," the senator started, "if I told you that I have access to a device that could spy on anyone, anywhere, *any time* in the past?"

"I would say," Muriel responded with her eyebrows high on her forehead, "that you're still hung over from one of those liquid lunches at the Senate Building."

"It's not funny, Muriel," Hopkins replied without a hint of a smile. "It's deadly serious, and I need your advice on what to do."

When Muriel said nothing, he continued. "I'm in a position to save our country from a potentially devastating tragedy, but the ethical considerations are so huge, I'm overwhelmed with indecision."

He proceeded to recount the whole story about Zack, the 'Time Scope', Petuccini, the experience of witnessing Kennedy's assassination and their agreement. He concluded by pointing out that he could spy on the past activities of Norman Brady, their party leader, and perhaps confirm his suspicion of this man's dictatorial ambitions.

"Muriel, help me sort this out in my head. There is no one whose judgement I respect more." He gazed into her face hopefully, but by now, it had lost all expression, as if carved from stone.

"Damn you, Gordon," she said very softly, almost inaudibly over the crackling of the fire in the huge Franklin stove. "I don't need the responsibility of helping you with this one." She added with some bitterness, "this is the kind of thing that destroyed our marriage twenty-four years ago. Do you want to risk our friendship as well?"

Gordon Hopkins did not reply. He knew that he had to wait for Muriel to make up her mind. He was prepared to go home without discussing his problem any further, if this is what she wanted. After a while, he saw her shoulders sag in defeat. She took a deep breath and looked him directly in the eyes.

"All right, then, if you must. What's your dilemma?"

Chapter 3

Zacharias Dougall, known to his friends as Zack, was pissed off. After he had installed the computer hookup for the power supply, programmed the computer to randomly generate two passwords and activate the relay switch only when they were entered correctly, he was unceremoniously locked out of his own room by Petuccini's 'serviceman'.

He knew that he had trapped himself into this situation, which did not make it any easier to tolerate. He was between a rock and a hard place, not quite sure which of his overseers was which. Both the senator and Petuccini were forces way beyond his level of competence. He just had to wait and see where all of this would lead.

He briefly considered discussing his situation with Suzy, but quickly changed his mind: that could be the last straw his girl needed to become his ex-girl.

Just wait, he told himself, *both of these 600 pound gorillas need my help and, if I play my cards right, I might get out of this not just alive, but even with something to show for all this shit I have to put up with.*

He had to deal with it one day at a time, and today was the first. The senator and the mobster were due to arrive soon, to run Petuccini's experimental 'research' on the newly configured system.

~

Petuccini was first, unaccompanied by his bodyguards.

"Hello, Zack," he greeted the morose young man. "Let's see if I can open this door for you?" He proceeded to insert a very peculiar key into the new lock and, without further ado, marched right in. Zack followed, not hiding his resentment over being a second-class citizen in his own home.

"Now, show me how this setup works. I would appreciate expediency, as my time is quite valuable."

It was all very simple. They had to turn on the power bar, which started all kinds of transformers in the room` buzzing, then booted up the laptop now wired into the network of cables that connected everything. The computer then displayed input boxes for the two passwords and, below them, a 'Start' button.

Both Petuccini and Hopkins had already had their own passwords generated and emailed to them by Zack's program. Of course, Zack had no problem finding out what these were, but he could not use them himself because he was locked out of the room unless this overbearing guest was present.

Hopkins soon arrived, deep in thought as usual. He was worried about another meeting with Petuccini, even at an obscure residence in the suburbs. *"What if a journalist finds out?"* He could never discount this possibility, but he thought it was worth taking this small risk.

His consultation with Muriel convinced him that he must proceed with the plan. Unfortunately, Petuccini had won the coin toss and he was forced to wait. Hopefully, it wouldn't take too long for 'Romeo' to find out what he wanted about his girlfriend, and then it would be his turn.

~

Before leaving Atlantic City, Petuccini had instructed Maria Montrose, the assistant manager of his "Dreams Come True Casino", to keep a close eye on the shop. Two problems were brewing in the background and he wanted to make sure that nothing would come to a head while he was in Washington. He had told her that he would be away for a week, not a long time for her to pull double shifts to ensure that everything was running smoothly, that nobody was causing any trouble.

He trusted her loyalty on the job, since it was Maria who had alerted him to the manager's improper handling of the slot machines, and undisclosed phone conversations with one of Petuccini's business rivals. There was no solid reason to doubt her sexual fidelity either - except that he never understood why she was attracted to him. He was middle aged, in reasonable shape, but no movie star. She was an absolute knockout, gorgeous thirty-five years old, she had an accounting degree, a solid career and no need for his money. Then *why*? Good looking hunks were abundant on the casino circuit and Petuccini wouldn't be surprised if Maria, being confident and adventurous, decided to sample all that his world could offer.

Maria did not object to his request, which was reassuring, but now he wanted to be sure that her nights had been as innocent as her very busy 16 hour workdays.

After the two passwords were entered and the machine came alive, he instructed Zack to tune the 'Space' dial to the GPS location of Maria's bedroom, and the 'Time' dial to 1AM, on the day after he'd left town for his visit to Washington.

When the Time Scope showed the scene, they could clearly see the bed occupied by one person and Petuccini recognized the sleeping face of his girl, her long dark brown hair spread out on the pillow. He watched her lovely face for a few minutes with deep satisfaction.

So far, so good.

He told Zack to hold the space coordinates, but keep changing the time randomly from midnight to 7AM, one day ahead each time, until they arrived at this morning.

On second try they caught her getting ready for bed, preparing to undress and change into her nightgown. Petuccini hastily ordered Zack to look the other way, while Senator Hopkins had already turned his back. Petuccini enjoyed watching her voluptuous body slowly released from her elegant pantsuit and far too quickly obscured again by her nightgown.

Repeating the random search, his two companions soon lost interest, because the result was always the same: Maria sleeping peacefully in her own bed at any time they looked throughout the night.

Petuccini was satisfied. He knew that Maria had a demanding job at the casino, a job that kept her busy all day and evening, in full public view or in the office with its security system, with no privacy at all, except during the night and, as he had just learned, her nights were as innocent as could be.

He stood up with a big sigh of relief, shook his head in wonder a few times and then laughed, maybe a bit too loudly, to hide his embarrassment. "Gentlemen," he announced, "I realize that my worries were unjustified, and now I have to ponder how to deal with my new-found situation."

Hopkins and Zack gazed at him with uncertainty, waiting for specifics.

Petuccini obliged. "I propose to set a date next week for the senator's session. I have some business to attend to in New Jersey that cannot be postponed."

"I hoped to do it sooner than that," Hopkins protested. "For me, every day increases the danger."

Petuccini was sympathetic but unbending. He ordered Zack to shut down the system and suggested they all leave the room, so that he could relock it.

After a brief hesitation, Hopkins accepted the decision and followed the others out of the room. The loud click of the lock emphasized the end of this incredibly unexciting time travel session they had experienced.

~

After a bumpy one hour flight, Joe Petuccini was greeted by Maria at Ocean City Airport. She thought that the brewing crises at the Casino required Joe's immediate attention and wanted to start reporting on business the second he arrived. However, her carefully prepared opening had no chance, because Joe was uncharacteristically emotional. He picked her up in the air and twirled her around, in plain sight of everyone.

"Babe, I missed you so much!" Joe enthused "What do you say we go straight to bed and make up for lost time?"

"What's got into you?" Maria gasped the words out and wriggled from his tight embrace, "It's only been a week!"

"A week, a day, who cares?" Petuccini dismissed her objections, and declared solemnly, "At my age, sweetheart, a week can seem an eternity without your sweet lips. Let us adjourn to my sanctum and correct this huge omission first. Then we may confer."

Maria was too impressed with her lover's enthusiasm to protest any longer. She wasted no more time, but drove him home to resume their mutually satisfactory relations. Petucinni derived a little secret pleasure from imagining himself on the other side of the time scope, looking in.

~

Hours later, after immediate emergencies were taken care of, she tried again to talk sense with him. "Joe, you have a problem here and you need to take care of it. John is really screwing you with the slot machines and maybe trying to sell you out to the Markos consortium. At least, I've caught him a couple of times, making secretive phone calls, while you were away."

Joe sobered up quickly. He had suspected something like this, but now Maria seemed to have some evidence, though not solid enough.

What should he do about it? Obviously, the same thing he had had to do, year after year, with upstarts who had become too bold for their own good. Suddenly, he felt overwhelmed by boredom - the "here we go again" kind that usually arrives on the doorstep of successful businessmen. They have seen it all, done it all before and there is no challenge left; no novelty to enjoy and look forward to.

Did he need more of this? How long was he going to keep repeating the same pattern? Is this the way he wanted to spend the rest of his life?

Here he was, in bed, with this fantastic, intelligent, loyal woman who, for a unfathomable reason, was attracted to him; who offered him a relationship such as he had never had before, and he was twisting his brain into a pretzel, trying to figure out how to deal with low-life vermin that did not deserve a minute of his attention.

He decided to sleep on it and enjoy the rest of the night in his own bed, in the arms of his own mistress, with his own secret of knowing everything about anyone's past if he so wished. He would need to think this all through.

His mind wandered over to the 'Time Scope'. What was it that the senator wanted? What was important enough to risk associating with a notorious character like himself? The senator had mentioned danger, but never explained what danger he meant, from what quarter.

According to their agreement, he had a right to know, and veto power over, the other man's purpose. He resolved to call the senator in the morning and move the date of their next session up a few days, to discuss the project and the procedure they were to follow. His domestic problem could wait a bit longer. He found this new situation very amusing, how the three of them, such drastically different personalities, found themselves allied in some kind of conspiracy. With this final thought, and decision, he kissed Maria good night and emptied his whirling mind, ready for much needed sleep.

~

Senator Hopkins didn't find sleep as easily as his exhausted 'partner'. He kept going over his worries regarding Norman Brady. He had no solid grounds for concern; only rumours, news reports, the man's own campaign speeches and - most importantly - his last conversation with the nominee.

At the end of a long night strategy session at party headquarters, Hopkins was reasonably sure that

Brady was sounding him out on the possibility of sharing the ticket. He had been more open and forceful in his questions than ever been before, and those questions were deeply troubling.

Perhaps Brady had been a little bit drunk at the time; maybe he wasn't aware of how much he'd revealed about his intentions, when, not if, he won the election and become president. He had demanded to know how Hopkins felt about governance, democracy and leadership.

"Gordon, what do you think is the biggest problem in our country?" Without waiting for a reply, he'd answered his own question. "Lack of strong leadership. All this stupid hand-wringing over civil rights, and legal jurisdiction and due process has paralyzed this country."

Hopkins waited for clarification.

"I don't mind admitting that I've always admired strong leaders. Sure, some of 'em were misguided, took the wrong direction. But they got things done, by God, and the government fell in behind them, or else! They unified their people."

Hopkins wanted more, so he asked: "For instance, Norman? Give me some examples."

"Don't take me wrong," Brady continued. "I despise some of the decisions they made and I know a couple of 'em went overboard, but you've got to respect the strength and the grit. Because those guys achieved what they had wanted to achieve."

Hopkins started to have very bad feelings about this. But Brady wasn't finished. "Just for their efficiency, and not their aims, I give credit to America's favourite whipping boys, like Saddam Hussein, Vladimir Putin, and, even way back, before we knew any better, even Hitler and Mussolini had their moments. *Somebody*'s got to make the trains run on time, eh?"

Gordon Hopkins was flabbergasted. He stared into the other's belligerent, alcohol-soaked glare and couldn't utter a sound. Brady must have sensed his shock, because he suddenly changed his tone, as if a switch was thrown, and laughed loudly at Hopkins.

"Gordon, you should see your face!" he guffawed. "You don't really think I'm serious? I was just kidding around, man! " He slapped Hopkins heartily on the back and walked away, shaking his head and chortling all the way to the bar.

Hopkins managed a weak smile and uttered an uncertain "No, I suppose not", to nobody, but found himself still reeling from the sudden revelation of the man's potentially terrifying intentions.

That was the end of their interview, if it was what he thought it was, and they never spoke of it again.

Chapter 4

Susan Turnbull was lonely. The Last time they met, she'd been quite harsh with Zack. She had wanted to jolt him out of his rut, not to hurt or discourage him. She really cared for him: his quirky ways were endearing and made her laugh, and the sex was terrific.

She had not seen him for over a week and he had not even tried to call once in that time. How had he reacted to her ultimatum? Was he making an effort to find a regular job? Or had he given up? Was she going to lose him? She decided to drop in after her shift at the "Geraniums" flower shop, where she was employed, nine to five, like a normal person. She hoped things were still OK between them.

When her boyfriend opened the door, Suzy was startled by his appearance: more unkempt than ever and no sign of his characteristic good cheer.

"Hi Zack, will you let me in? Unless you don't want to see me any more after the way I talked to you?"

"Suzy! I do want to see you!" The words tumbled out of Zack in a rush. "I didn't expect it but I'm happy you came. Boy, am I *ever* ! Come in!"

"What's wrong?" Susan asked, not quite sure what gave her the impression that he was in some kind of trouble.

Zack led the way back to his living room and sat down on his usual spot on the sofa, while Susan took the chair. She looked around the room, searching for clues to his morose demeanor, and almost immediately noticed the shiny new deadlock on his workshop door.

"What the hell, Zack?" she exclaimed. "What do you need *that for*?"

Zack emitted a big sigh, realizing that he had no choice but to tell Susan everything. All through his exposition, her eyes grew larger and larger, her expression slowly changed from suspicious incredulity to something near horror.

"So, I am locked out of my own lab by a senator and a gangster," Zack concluded his tale, "and I have no idea what's going to happen." He added softly. "I'm a bit scared, kind of pissed, and super frustrated. I don't know how to get free of these guys."

It took her a while to digest this incredible story, but the lock on the door and Zack's worried, almost grown-up, face convinced her that it was for real. *A time-scope? Spying on people's activities anywhere, any time in the past?* If she believed that, she'd believe anything.

Her practical, no-nonsense mind finally prevailed over her emotional turmoil and began to consider the actual situation. "Why do you let them push you around?" she demanded. "Didn't you tell me that they couldn't use it without you?"

"Yes, I know, but…"

"Don't be such a wuss, for crying out loud!" Suzan exclaimed. "Have you tried to set your own terms?"

"What terms?"

"I don't know, You're the genius with the gadget. *You* found this time scope or whatever you want to call it. *You* figured out how to use it. You're the one who can operate it ."

"That's all true, but…"

"Well then, it makes sense that you should get some benefit from it, not just be a servant to those big important bozos. I hate to see them walk all over you!"

"Yeah! So, how do I do that?"

"Think, Zack! What could you use it for? Trying to blackmail a senator was the dumbest idea you ever had, and that's what dropped you in this pile of shit."

"Hey! Be fair. I did *not* try to blackmail him!" Zack protested. "I only wanted to help clear his name, so I could use him as a reference."

"You mean, for a job?" she asked hopefully.

"Um, no. I was thinking of, maybe, setting up a private detective agency. Solving crimes and mysteries that nobody else could. I'd have no competition at all."

Susan was impressed, seeing the potential in this scheme.

"That would kill several birds with one stone," she admitted. "You wouldn't have to hold down a regular job, you could do most of your work at home, tinker with your toys and pull a fairly steady income."

"Suzy, I love the idea," he confessed, "but how can I start? I'm locked out and can't do a damn thing without their permission. I can't get them off my back."

"Zack, be a man. Stand up on your hind legs!" Suzy replied angrily. "Next time they come, tell them that you won't help their research any more unless they let you do your own." Seeing Zack was ready to object, she added hastily, "Make sure they understand that you'll only use it for legitimate business, that they can monitor everything you do, but that's the deal – take it or leave it."

"Do you think I could get away with this?" Zack asked with a glimmer of hope appearing on his lugubrious face.

"What have you got to lose?" his girl asked in exasperation, which evaporated as she thought of a possible answer. "Anyway, you'll never find, unless you ask."

"I guess you're right," Zack nodded slowly, combing his long fingers through his hair in thought. "So that's what I'll do." He was silent a moment, then shyly asked: "Is the couch too uncomfortable to fool around on? You know it's been... a while."

Susan rolled her eyes. "I thought you'd never ask".

~

Petuccini and Hopkins arrived almost at the same time. Zack greeted them with great apprehension, but fully determined to follow Suzy's advice: she had made him promise to stand up for himself, with dire threats concerning their relationship if he didn't.

He looked at them defiantly and declared, in a somewhat shaky voice: "Before we do anything, I have to clarify my role in this enterprise."

The other two stared back at him.

Petuccini appreciated the humour in the situation: it was as if a chair had spoken up and demanded fair treatment. "You are in no position, young man, to clarify or negotiate. Your role is to avoid jail, or worse."

Zack had had enough. His boiling point was unusually high, but the frustration of the last two weeks and then the contempt in Petuccini's voice pushed him over the top. "That goes for all three of us, I believe, unless you mean to make me disappear, so I can't testify against you for spying and god only knows what else you're planning here."

Petuccini burst out laughing at this unexpected show of temper. "Senator, would you believe this? The young fellow has spunk."

Hopkins wasn't amused. The illegality of what he had been contemplating weighed heavily on his mind and he did not care to be reminded.

"Maybe we should hear him out?" he suggested and, after a few seconds of considering, Petuccini agreed.

"Okay, let us humour him, if it doesn't take too long. We have important topics to discuss. All right, kid, you have the floor. Tell us concisely what you are after."

Zack was grateful to the senator and for the first time since they arrived, he actually saw hope.

"It's very simple," he started. "I found this device, I managed to make it work, I understood what it was for and how to use it, so I believe I'm entitled to some benefit from it, instead of being treated, in my own house, like a slave."

"You should have considered your options before trying to blackmail a US senator," Petuccini responded. "Let alone spying on me."

Zack shouted defiantly: "I was *not* trying blackmail! I never asked for money, and cooperated with the senator from the start. And I never spied on anybody except your girlfriend."

Hopkins couldn't deny this: "It's true. Zack did nothing improper. He offered to help me and I promised to help him."

Still Petuccini wasn't pacified. "He should have known better," he muttered.

Zack had only one card left and he was very reluctant to play it. Whichever way he put it, this would sound like blackmail, or extortion, as Petuccini would recognize instantly. He had to try something else first, before resorting to his final argument. "Okay, so, I'll go on helping with your research, as much as you like, but I want to be able to use it myself, too. Legitimately, of course. I've got to make a living. "

Now Petuccini was curious – he could not imagine a legitimate business connected to a spying machine.

Zack declared proudly: "I intend to start up as a private eye and work on unsolved crimes and mysteries. With this device, I could follow clues back in time and find out exactly what happened."

"I'll be damned!" Hopkins exclaimed, unable to hide his surprise and sudden realization of how well suited this innocent looking TV set was for criminal investigation.

Petuccini, in his turn, burst out laughing, unable to stop.

"Kid," he declared, "you *are* a genius!"

"Does that mean," Zack asked hopefully, "that you'll let me use it for this purpose?"

Petuccini and the senator looked at each other, the first still amused, the other in a thoughtful way.

"We need to think about it, Zack," Hopkins finally spoke up. "I don't think that your request is unreasonable, but we need to make sure that we have clear rules on who, when and how can have access to this device."

Petuccini seemed to be in agreement, or at least he did not outright veto the idea, so Zack felt encouraged to carry on.

"What I suggest, for a start, is that you remove that lock from my workshop door, because I can't get started without unlimited access to the very foundation of my plan." Before either of his 'guests' could interrupt, he added hastily, "However, I'm here 24/7 – something that neither of you can afford, so I can help with your own research and collect data on a regular basis for both of you – if you tell me what you are after."

"Now that's an idea!" Petuccini admitted.

"This way," Zack continued, "I can be your research assistant even while working on my own investigation."

Hopkins thought that this was a tremendous idea. Being a good judge of characters, he was tempted to trust Zack. Also, he'd never felt good about meeting regularly with Petuccini; it was only a question of time before some nosy reporter followed him to the house and noticed the other visitor. "I am inclined to go along with this," he said, looking over at Petuccini expectantly.

"Very well. I will give it a try, young man," his 'partner' looked at Zack sternly. "But you would very much regret trying to pull a fast one on either of us."

Zack's sigh of relief could have launched a commuter flight.

"I won't let you down, either of you!" he promised. "I'll be an enthusiastic assistant in whatever plans you two have." He couldn't resist elaborating, "Much better for all of us if I don't participate with reluctance and resentment."

"Okay, kid," Petuccini decided. "The lock stays until such time as we ascertain that we can trust you." Before Zack could protest, he added, "but I won't lock it any more unless," he raised a warning finger "you give me reason to do so."

~

Norman Brady was livid. These goddamn journalists were picking up every fucking scrap of gossip they could lay their hands on. Nobody appreciated what a miracle he had achieved by securing his nomination, in their stupid faces, in spite of all their educated guesses and projections.

Everybody kept parroting that the people wanted change and, by God, he was going to give them change – the kind they had never seen before in America. No more bullshit excuses, no half measures, he was going full out and nobody could stop him.

His followers were enthusiastic, pumped-up, motivated. All you had to do was appeal to their fear, greed and, most of all their hatred of anything you told them threatened their grubby little existence.

Brady was a salesman - the best of his kind. He knew what made people tick and what they wanted to hear. No point telling them what they did not want to hear. Truth had nothing to do with it. Politics wasn't about telling the truth, it was about scoring points on your opponents.

But the fucking bastards just kept coming after him, questioning his credentials, his accomplishments, his methods. It was infuriating that he had to tolerate them a little while longer.

He'd have to make a decision very soon about a running mate. His plan for Hopkins fell through when he realized that Gordon was too much of a boy scout. Too bad, because a boy scout would have looked good on the ticket, would have mollified some of his critics.

Anyway, time to think about going to bed, it was nearly 3AM, he'd just finished updating his Facebook, sent out his last emails and could call it a day. The fundraising was going well and even some of the party brass started to fall in line. All in all, it was looking good.

~

Muriel spent a sleepless night after Gordon's visit. His shocking revelation about their party leader, coupled with the fantastic news about a spying machine, deeply disturbed her. She had been a politician's wife long enough to realize how much damage a rogue president could do to the country and, for this reason, she encouraged Gordon to pursue his investigation.

Which was not without danger, she realized. Whatever Gordon managed to discover about Brady's past activities, how on earth could he make it public? He couldn't just announce the existence of the 'Time Scope', they both agreed. Without that evidence he had no case and would only make things worse – the backlash would be devastating. She fully realized the quandary he was in. Could he find out something that might compel Brady to withdraw from the race? Maybe just letting him know, anonymously, that somebody was on to him?

Muriel still deeply cared for Gordon and wanted to help him through these difficult times. What if she put her own projects on hold and traveled to Washington to be with him for moral support? One problem though: she had two dogs she refused to put in a kennel. Bearcub and Daisy were very attached to her and she could not contemplate leaving them with strangers.

However, Gordon was also very fond of dogs and he did live alone in a house with a little yard; there might be room for them. She decided to leave it up to him, and quickly, before she could think better of it, sent off an email message to his home address:

"Gordon, I have some business in Washington this coming week and, if you think you could put me up for a few days, with two of my dependents, please let me know."

She has done all she could, the rest was up to him.

Chapter 5

Gordon Hopkins, United States senator, wasn't sure what he'd gotten himself into. He wasn't supposed to be here. He could face severe punishment if it ever became public. Yet, he couldn't leave. The stakes were too high. He had to know the truth about Brady.

All Hopkins knew, even after extensive research, was that Petuccini had never been in prison, had never been indicted; though he had been investigated, there was no criminal record on file. He was third generation Mafia, his ill reputation seemed to come from his family connections, rather than what he had actually done. He had kept himself busy for years, running a major casino and convention center in Ocean City and was not involved in anything else, as far as Hopkins could tell. The only allegations of underworld activity appeared in gossip columns.

Not enough to scare Hopkins away, but certainly not something a US Senator could advertise in his next re-election campaign.

According to their agreement, he was duty bound to explain his project to Petuccini, and he had no idea of the other's political leaning, or how he would react. Still, it had to be done, and he briefly outlined the background to his worries and the information he needed.

To his surprise, Petuccini was enthusiastic. "Senator, you may find it strange that a man like me is interested in politics." He shook his head as if trying to dislodge some nasty insects. "As a matter of fact, I am not," he continued, "but nor am I altogether oblivious to what transpires in this country – *our* country."

Hopkins raised an inquiring eyebrow.

"That poseur, your party's nominee, his braggadocio about being a self-made man, that makes my blood boil!" He almost shouted the last sentence. "I could tell him something about self-made men – people who did not start out with a trust fund from their papa!"

There was no doubt in Hopkins' whom Petuccini had in mind.

"He claims to be tough on immigration and crime, but all he wants to do is make poor people's lives harder, while he and his confederates grow even richer." He stared at Hopkins intently, as if trying to convince him of something the senator already knew. "It is easy to talk tough when one has an army at his command and no gun in his own face. If you want to dig up any dirt on the bastard, I am all for it."

"That's settled then." Hopkins sighed with relief, and proceeded to lay out his plan.

He wanted to start a thorough investigation on Brady's comings and goings and even his home activities. He asked Zack to film meetings that Brady had with everyone who visited and any private conferences he had. Hopkins would review the footage once a week, and give Zack further instructions as required.

When all the questions were answered and all the clarifications given, Hopkins and Petuccini left, a few minutes apart.

~

Zack had been locked out of his workshop so long that he couldn't wait to step inside. Everything was exactly as they left it, except that, without the stultifying presence of his two chaperones, it felt roomier. Finally, he was master in his own house again, not a criminal on probation.

He walked over to his 'Time Scope' and gently placed his hand on top of the box, caressing it affectionately. He would start working soon, after he had called Suzy. She had made him promise that this would be the first item on his agenda the minute his visitors left.

"Hi Zack, how did it go?"

"Amazing! I still can't believe it - we *won!* They went for the deal and I didn't even have to use blackmail!"

"That's great! So what are you going to do now?"

"I really want to try that private eye business, but I don't exactly know how to get started," Zack admitted reluctantly.

"Why don't you Google unsolved crime rewards?" Suzy suggested, giving Zack the impression that she had already considered the same question at some length. "That way you can have a guaranteed income - assuming you produce the evidence and collect."

"That's a great idea, Suzy. I'll get right on it."

"You want me to come over?" she asked, a bit too eagerly for Zack's liking.

"No, Hon, not this time. I want to try it on my own. You've been a terrific help, but I need to figure things out for myself."

"Okay. Let me know how it's going," she said and rang off.

~

When Hopkins got home and looked at his email, he found Muriel's brief note about a visit to Washington. Good thing he was sitting down; this was a shock. They had not slept under the same roof since their divorce twenty-four years ago and he was not sure what her message implied.

The "business in Washington" part was too much of a coincidence to believe. Therefore, he could imagine only two possible explanations. Either Muriel wanted to rekindle their old love, that he was sure still lingered under the ashes, or she believed in his dangerous plan and wanted to give him advice and a shoulder to lean on. For his own peace of mind, he chose to believe the latter.

He had been introduced to the dogs on his recent visit, and he had no objection to having them around for a few days. He looked at the open email one more time, and then replied:

"Dear Muriel, I'd be delighted to put you up for a few days and don't worry about your dependents. Bring whatever they need, or I can lay in some dog food if you tell me the brand. I'm sure we can find dishes around the house. Let me know when you plan to arrive and I'll pick you up at the airport."

Rereading it one more time, he clicked on the 'Send' button and watched the slider bar delivering his message. For better or worse, now he was committed.

~

Zack was just about to start searching for his first client when the doorbell rang. Would Suzy come over on a week-day? he wondered.

He was disappointed to find Petuccini on his doorstep, smiling mysteriously.

"I guess you didn't expect me back so soon, kid," the big man said. "I must remain in Washington a few days longer and I have a business proposition for you."

Zack was taken aback. The change of demeanor in his feared persecutor was unbelievable. He barely managed to stammer out: "What are you talking about? What kind of business?"

Petuccini pushed past him into his living room, and Zack had no choice but to follow. His visitor sat down in his usual armchair and looked him up and down appraisingly, as if trying to determine whether he could be entrusted with a job.

Zack sat down on his sofa and waited.

"I know that it's the senator's turn," Petuccini began. "However, there is nothing in our agreement prohibiting a separate contract between you and I."

"Like what?" Zack blurted out, losing patience.

"You will be doing the senator's research but, you could also investigate something for me."

"You don't mean you actually want to hire me as a private eye?" Now this really was a change in their relationship!

"Yes, this is precisely what I do mean." Petuccini continued, "and there is financial reward, if you find the evidence I require."

"Money?" Zack's eyebrows ran up to his hairline. "How much?"

"How does five grand sound?"

Zack was speechless; he could only nod several times, while swallowing hard.

"I take it," Petuccini smiled, "that your nodding means 'yes'. Then, I shall indicate what I am after."

Zack fished out the notebook and pen he always carried in his shirt pocket.

Petuccini explained how he had deep suspicions that his manager was conspiring with a rival to sabotage his slot machines and trigger massive financial losses that would force him to sell at a loss. He needed proof on video tape that two men, John Wasserman and Jose Markos, had met secretly, more than once, during the last month.

He gave Zack both office and home locations, two snapshots and the time period to investigate. He suggested tracking Wasserman as the easier mark.

"I will need it fairly soon, if you do secure evidence," he concluded. "This is my mobile number," he gave Zack a business card. "Call me when you have something."

~

Reading Gordon's invitation, Muriel almost lost her nerve. *What am I getting into?* She asked herself, and then repeated the question to Daisy, who joined her at the desk, placing a warm muzzle on her knee, in reminder that it was time for their daily romp in the forest.

Muriel wasn't ready yet. Gordon asked for a flight number. But that would be too stressful for the dogs, who had never been in an airplane. She looked up the Montpelier to Washington route and learned that it is 583 miles via the I 91; estimated travel time 9 hours. With judicious speeding, she could cut it down to include necessary stops to walk and water the dogs. A whole day's drive: if she left early in the morning, she could get there by late afternoon or early evening.

The idea of having her own car on the visit appealed to Muriel: she would be independent, not have to rely on Gordon, public transit or taxis for transportation.

Besides, the long drive would be an excellent opportunity to mull things over. She had to determine which was more important to her: to spend time with Gordon again, after so many years apart, or to provide encouragement. Apparently, Gordon wasn't the only one who needed it.

Decisions made, she dashed off a reply to Gordon, advising him of the day and time to expect her arrival, by car instead of plane; that saved him a trip to the airport.

"Okay, Daisy, *now* it's time to go." She stood up and followed her out to the front porch where Bearcub was already prancing in place under the leashes hanging from their hook. "If I get into trouble, kids," she admonished, "it will be your fault. You didn't talk me out of it."

~

"I'll tell you the whole story," she addressed her two companions on the back seat, who were hanging on every word. "Gordon and I met at Johnson State College, in residence. He was in the Bachelor of Science program, I was in Fine Arts. We were both far from home, shy and lonely."

"He was charming and intelligent and not bad looking so, as time went by, we became good friends. Very good friends. We planned, after graduation, to build a house outside town on some nice treed lot and live happily ever after.

"It worked out fairly well. He got a job with Honeywell in Montpelier and I started selling a few landscapes, getting commissions… Sculpture went even better, and once I began working in wood – well you know how that's going!

"Then, things got complicated. Gordon became involved in politics. He felt passionate about one issue, then another… Seeing all the unfairness and inequality, he had to do something. He ran for councillor, then the state legislature and, finally got elected into his current position: senior senator for the state of Vermont.

"Are you two still with me?"

Daisy and Bearcub almost nodded their heads in unison.

"Okay, then, I'll go on," Muriel said, trying to determine how much she wanted to admit to her two friends, or maybe to herself. "That's when our problems started. Gordon wanted to move to Washington, as his job required, and I was horrified at the prospect of leaving our beautiful house in the woods for a big city. My art would have suffered and I would have had to give it up.

"I flatly refused to go and he had to choose. For a while, he kept coming home on weekends and summer vacations, but these became fewer and shorter as the years went by.

"That was a very long time ago," she explained, "way before you were born. Eventually, we realized that living apart had become a permanent arrangement. Neither of us wanted to be dishonest. We decided on a divorce to free us to find more suitable mates, without trauma or guilt."

"Years, then decades went by, but we managed to stay good friends. Even though we had other romantic attachments in our lives, we never really stopped caring for each other."

She added with a sigh:

"Now we're both free again and I have to admit: I'm a bit lonely without a human companion. You guys can't make up for the stimulating intellectual conversations I enjoyed with Gordon.

"The big question I'm asking myself - and you two as well, so pay attention: Will I let myself get involved with him again? If I do, beware, that is not without danger. The conflict of interest is still there: he's still a senator, and I would never leave my house in the woods, so you can relax. What do you think?"

Her furry friends on the back seat, after brief consultation, responded that as long as they could get out of this noisy, stinky car, they would go along with anything she suggested.

Chapter 6

Zack wasn't sure where to start. He had two assignments, one paid, the other voluntary, if you could call it that. Thinking about it, he realized that Petuccini's task was the easier: he had to find out if those people had actually met. How hard could it be with his 'Time Scope'?

He looked up both addresses on Google Earth to obtain the space coordinates, then set up a random search pattern at the two locations, at different times on different days, hoping to get lucky and spot either one leaving or arriving.

After two days of staring at the monitor, Zack decided to automate the process and save himself from the crimped neck that was fast developing. His computer had face-recognition software, so he scanned in the two photos Petuccini had given him and aimed the computer's high resolution camera at the screen of the 'Time Scope'. Programming the software to sound an audio alarm if a match was found was no problem at all.

Now he could relax and let his gadgets do the work.

He was warming up his TV dinner when the phone rang.

"Hi Zack, how is it going?" Suzy's voice was full of excitement and anticipation.

"I just got started and it's too early to tell, but you won't believe what I'm working on!" He couldn't resist bragging about his first paying job.

"Zack, that's wonderful! I'm so happy for you!" she enthused. "Can I come over and watch? Please? Pretty please?"

Zack didn't have the heart to say no; besides, he was ready to resume their activity on the sofa of a few days ago.

She arrived half an hour later.

Zack explained the setup and how it was automated, so they would have time for some fun while the computer watched the screen.

"That's men for you," Susan sighed in exasperation, "They'll do anything to avoid work!"

"You don't think 'fun' could be work? I think it's hard aerobic exercise. Good for your health!"

Before Susan could answer, a loud beep from the computer made them rush over to the 'Time Scope'. They got there barely in time for Zack to zoom in on the moving figure and press the 'Track' knob.

John Wasserman walked across the parking lot and got in his car. The 'Time Scope' followed him to a nearby strip mall, apparently to buy something at the pharmacy, and then drive back to his office in the casino.

"That sucks!" Susan sounded disappointed.

"You can't expect to hit the jackpot on the first try," Zack cautioned. "This will take some time. I've been watching this guy for two days now and it might take another two before I catch him red-handed."

"Or not," Susan was still morose, seeing no immediate result. "I guess you just have to keep doing it. At least you don't get gum on your shoes with this setup," she giggled. "So, what do you want to do now?"

"You know what I want to do now," Zack rolled his eyes, liberated two bottles of Labatt's beer from the fridge and turned on the music as he passed his stereo. He had prepared for her arrival the minute she said she was coming.

This became an enjoyable routine for both of them in the following evenings, only interrupted by the occasional beep from the computer when the software recognized one or the other of his quarries on the screen.

Before each new session, Zack adjusted the space and time coordinates, alternating between the two addresses. If Petuccini's suspicion was justified, sooner or later, he was bound to record some action. It took two more evenings of diligent watching before something happened. They were tracking Markos as he drove to a different plaza from the one where he usually shopped. They saw him pull into the parking lot, and then sit in his car. After a short while, a dark green Toyota parked beside him and the driver, a young man with blond hair, joined Markos on the passenger seat. Before they could identify the face, the computer beeped again. It was Petuccini's manager. They had confirmation of the meeting; all they needed now was to prove it.

Zack didn't know if he could zoom close enough to the windshield to see both faces together, but he tried and finally got a clear picture. With his camera already mounted on a tripod, he filmed the two in animated conversation.

"If only I had lip-reading software," Zack shook his head regretfully, "I could find out what they're talking about."

After a few minutes of filming, he saw the men shake hands and part company. Zack quickly panned back and had a good shot of the two cars side by side, making sure it included a clear image of both license plates. From the 'Time' knob he copied down the actual date and time when the meeting took place.

"The money's in the bank, Suzy," Zack said mischievously. "What do you say we celebrate in style?"

Suzy chased him to the sofa and jumped into his lap, kissing his triumphant face. "Don't you have another assignment from the senator to start on?" she teased. They both knew that they had other plans for the rest of the evening.

~

Petuccini was impressed. The video Zack had given him was conclusive evidence of his manager's betrayal. Now he had to decide how to handle it. Suddenly, he realized what he wanted to do more than anything: discuss it with Maria - preferably after the reunion they usually enjoyed following a trip of more than a few days. Three hours later, back in his own bedroom, he did exactly that.

"That low-life! That rotten snake!" she exclaimed. "He owes you everything, after you gave him a job when nobody else would! You trusted him and this is how he repays you!"

After a few minutes of calming herself, she asked the simple question that Petuccini had been asking himself all the way home from Washington. "What are you going to do?"

"I don't know, Maria, I can't make up my mind and that's what bothers me most."

"Well, how about: you fire the bastard, put Carlos in charge for a couple of weeks and go away with me on a vacation, so you can really think it over without undue haste?"

"A vacation? I haven't had one of those for a long time," Petuccini said wistfully. "Do you think it would be wise?"

"Wiser than making an impulsive decision that may affect your whole life." Maria replied. "It's almost winter and I've heard that Porto Vallarta is particularly pretty this time of the year."

"I have to think, but it sounds very attractive," Petuccini admitted. "First I have to kick that creep out and then choose someone to put in his place temporarily. Carlos is a good idea, he will do for a few weeks. I have already got my choice for permanent replacement."

"You *have*?" Maria's eyes opened wide. "Do I know him?"

"It is a 'her' and you know her every time you look in the mirror," Joe chuckled at his own witticism, enjoying Maria's open-mouthed reaction to the announcement he had been planning for the last two weeks.

Finally, when she found her voice again, she asked more timidly than Joe had heard her speak before. "Are you sure? You think I can handle it, and not because we're... you know?"

"There is only one way to find out, cara, and you better not let me down."

"I'll do my best, but I think we really ought to take that vacation. After, we'll both start with a clean slate and a clear mind."

"Amen!" he agreed and that was the end of serious discussion for that evening.

~

Gordon Hopkins kept looking at the wall clock in his living room. He expected her any minute now and still wasn't sure how he would react to this exciting, disturbing and downright scary event that was about to take place. Muriel, in his own house, and no telling what it could lead to. They were in their late sixties, living alone. *Do we have to stay that way? What if old feelings still have a chance? What if Muriel feels the same way? What if she doesn't?*

He looked at the clock again, wondering where she might be, when the doorbell rang. He jumped up and hurried to the front door, expecting her, but found himself face to face with two large dogs, anxious to get inside, even if it involved knocking him off his feet.

Muriel tried to hold them back but she was no match for Bearcub: a hundred and twenty pound Great Pyrenees wasn't going to be stopped by a hundred and fifteen pound old lady.

"I'm so sorry, Gordon!" she apologized. "You better let them out to the yard, before they go through the wall. They've been cooped up in the car so long that they need to be free for a while."

Gordon saw the wisdom in that and opened the patio door to two very eager dogs, who wasted no time getting outside to water his lawn.

"Come in Muriel," he invited. "Can I help with your luggage?"

When everything was inside and carried upstairs to the guest room, he offered her the drink he knew was badly needed after such a long journey. One large scotch for himself, and a gin and tonic for Muriel, took only a minute to pour and finally they sat on his leather couch, facing each other. Each waited for the other to start talking, and then they both spoke at once, leading to an embarrassed laugh that broke the mood of apprehension.

"Isn't it like old times?" she asked and then added, "with one big difference: we're both a lot older and wiser."

"I don't know about the wiser part," Gordon confessed, "but I agree about the older bit: my knees and my back tell me daily."

They had some idle chit-chat about her trip that gave them time to compose and organize their faces and their feelings.

"Tell me what's happening." Muriel started.

He briefly explained the new arrangement with the other two conspirators, adding that he now had a research assistant, so his exposure became significantly smaller, not having to meet with Petuccini or visit Zack's house more than once a week.

"I instructed him to look into Brady's activities and meetings for the last month, to find anything that I should know."

"There must be something," Muriel commented, "because the way he's been talking on the campaign sounds wilder and scarier every day."

"I know. It sounds to me, and to a lot of my friends on the hill, as if he were gearing up for some kind of war, or revolution or I don't know what. His supporters are so crazy, anything can happen if he becomes president - as seems more and more likely." Gordon acknowledged with deep creases on his forehead, throwing his hands up in the air. "I'm preparing for the worst. He seems unstoppable, unless Zack finds something that I can use."

"Let's hope he does," Muriel sighed. "But we can't do anything about it tonight."

Gordon suddenly remembered: "I haven't asked if you if you're hungry! I can warm up something."

"Thanks, I had a quick dinner on the way, so all I need now is sleep."

"Oh, you must be very tired," Gordon apologized. "Flying all the time, I forget how long a drive that is. Go straight to bed!"

"Yes, that would be wise, only, I need to feed the dogs first. Would you mind letting them sleep in my room? They'd feel insecure unless I was within sight and smell."

"No problem, I just put an old rug on the floor, so they can lie on it more comfortably than on the bare wood."

"Thanks. I hope we won't be too much trouble. Tomorrow we can discuss everything else we need to, but I admit, right now, I'm really bushed."

With that, they felt they had said everything that they were prepared to say and, after a shy and cursory hug, they went about their evening ablutions.

Tomorrow, they both thought, *maybe tomorrow we discuss this very strange experience of being together, under the same roof again, after almost three decades.*

Chapter 7

Norman Brady was increasingly annoyed with his campaign manager. Trevor Smyth was OK for organizing events, but he didn't have a clue how to motivate people. He wanted to play it safe, like everyone else, the same traditional shit people were fed up to the teeth with.

"Look Trevor," Brady tried one more time. "Let's be clear on who's running this show."

"I thought I was in charge of the campaign. I assumed that was my job." Trevor rubbed his forehead with the back of his hand, trying to steady his nerves at the same time.

"Your job description says," Brady chuckled, "I know, because I wrote it: to do what I tell you to do. Now I'm telling you to get off my back."

"So, you won't change your speech for tonight's rally?" Trevor was aghast. "You'll scare them to death!"

"Or I'll whip them into a frenzy they haven't seen since World War Two."

"But, how will it affect our allies? And what about Russia? And China? They'll be outraged at your foreign policy initiatives."

"Let 'em be outraged," Brady shrugged. "At least my actions, once I'm president, won't come as a complete surprise. It's time someone stood up and had some guts. We've been asleep too long, it's time to show them what we can do".

Trevor was shaking now. His boss frightened him more and more as the campaign progressed from one fiery speech to the next. He saw that it was hopeless, trying to steer Brady into a more moderated strategy. He began to wonder if it was too late to bail out.

"Trevor, you don't understand. You're not a general." Brady tried to explain to this clueless civilian. "I am. Four stars. I know what it takes to get results, and it's not pussyfooting and fence-sitting." His voice rose in pitch as memories of past frustrations came back to him. "I was restrained far too many times by chickenshit politicians! When a little courage and perseverance would have led us to victory, we had to endure humiliating defeat or stalemate."

"But do you think it's wise to alarm people? You could lose a lot of votes!"

"If I give them a vision of greatness, I motivate them. They'll vote for me".

"I know, but…"

"Have you noticed, Trevor, this is how you start most sentences lately?"

"What do you mean?"

"You've become a 'yes-I-know-but' guy and I'm tired of the 'but' part. Cut it out!"

With that order, Brady turned his back on his befuddled manager, leaving Trevor to see himself out.

Once alone, he went down the back hall, unlocked his private office. He reviewed the conversation in his mind and nodded with satisfaction. He'd controlled his voice sufficiently. Trevor had no idea of the depth of his disgust with the system he had served under for so long.

Being yanked back on the leash, like an impotent attack dog, by incompetent civilians, when I was on the verge of victory!

The thought was accompanied by a burning hatred for those with no right to call themselves leaders.

When I'm president, I'll show them real leadership. Just wait a bit more, push the right buttons in the right sequence, and then I'll be able to make a difference. My kind of difference.

He turned to The Map and resumed work on it.

~

Gordon and Muriel sat in silence in his breakfast nook, watching the two dogs sniff around the cedar fence surrounding the small back yard.

"They can't help it," Muriel said apologetically. "They're used to more running space where we…where I live."

"What did you say?" Gordon, startled from his reverie, tried to reconnect with the present. "Sorry, I was thinking about Brady's speech last night".

"I can't blame you, it petrified me too!" Muriel sighed.

"What was he thinking? Has he gone mad? You can't say things like that in an American Presidential election campaign! What's he trying to do, start World War Three?"

"I wouldn't be surprised if the Russians were preparing for it right now." Muriel shook her head and picked up the morning paper and read a quote from Brady's speech at the Orlando rally.

'It's time to assert ourselves as the only superpower left on the planet and stop the cowardly acceptance of rogue states like North Korea and Iran.'

What the hell does he mean by that?"

"Or this one." Gordon took the paper from her hand.

"'The American military is the most powerful in the world but we've had to fight with our arms tied behind our backs all through history. We must acknowledge our superiority instead of apologizing for it. We should use it to establish peace and order on this chaotic planet for the prosperity of our own people!'

This sounds like he's planning world conquest!" Gordon shook his head in disbelief. "And you know what scares me most? His supporters loved every word and seemed ready to attack anyone he pointed a finger at."

"You and your spy boy had better dig up something to use against that dangerous lunatic, or nobody may be able to stop him." Muriel said in a hushed, somber voice Gordon had not heard since the Cuban missile crisis.

~

Zack slept in. After the previous night's celebration with Suzy, dancing around the table with Petuccini's cheque in the middle, he was still groggy, having only a vague recollection of how the night ended.

Senator Hopkin's voice on the phone woke him up fast. He had almost forgotten about the assignment he had been 'volunteered' for.

"Zack, I need to talk to you today," Hopkins said in a serious tone. "I'll be calling on you after lunch," he announced and hung up.

"Who was it?" Suzy asked, coming out of the bathroom, wearing his shirt and nothing else.

"I didn't know you were still here. Don't you have to go to work?"

"Are you still drunk?" Suzy asked "it's my rare weekend off, and you did ask me to stay over."

"Oh, sorry, it's coming back to me now," Zack confessed sheepishly. "that was Senator Hopkins. He's coming over. I've got to do some work on his project, double-quick, and I don't think you should be here when he arrives. Might be classified info," he added with a wink.

Susan rolled her eyes. "You guys and your secrets! Don't worry, I have better things to do with my weekend than cloak and dagger stuff."

Gordon Hopkins found Zack ready to proceed, sitting in his workshop, computer and the 'Time Scope' turned on, notepad and pen in hand. He was pleased by the young man's sudden attention and serious demeanor, because he wanted to impress upon him the importance of his assignment.

He briefly explained what to look for and why, and pointed out that Zack was in a position to avert a major disaster for their country.

Zack, not much aware of political reality, nevertheless perceived the danger posed by the quotes from Brady's speech that Hopkins read out to him. He promised to start immediately and record everything suspicious.

~

Petuccini and Maria were doing something neither had ever done before: riding horses. In a Mexican forest, following a bunch of tourists uphill, toward a spectacular waterfall. At least, that's what their Mexican guide promised. He'd even showed an old black and white snapshot of the falls, with the cross of a diving figure in front of it, arms outstretched, half way down to the small pool at the bottom.

"That's me, jumping!" he announced proudly. "You and I jump together," he grinned and nudged Petuccini in the ribs. "Great fun, you see!"

Petuccini laughed in a carefree way Maria had never heard before.

"I think I will watch you do it," he told Santos. "It will be safer!"

He must have impressed the guide when he had asked for straight tequila, instead of the various mixed drinks other tourists ordered on the boat ride across the bay. With a mysterious smile, Santos had brought out a full bottle. He unscrewed the cap and dropped a small pebble in, then handed it to Petuccini.

"You get pebble out, you keep whole bottle," he challenged.

"How?" Petuccini asked.

"I show you." Santos said. He tilted the bottle up to his lips and, after a second, showed it to the American. The pebble was gone. Santos spat it into his hand, then dropped it back into the tequila. "Now you do it."

Petuccini tried. He raised the bottle up as Santos had, waited till he could feel the pebble against his lip, cautiously opened his mouth - and promptly got his face washed with tequila. But the pebble stayed where it was.

"Neat trick, I have to practice it at home." By that time many of the other tourists were watching the show and laughed good naturedly at Petuccini's failure. He joined in.

"Joe, I've never seen you this happy before." Maria remarked, when everyone stopped listening. "You should seriously consider doing this more often!"

"I have been thinking the same," her lover admitted. "What's the point of being rich if I don't take the time to enjoy the benefits? I will give it more thought when we get home, I promise!"

The two weeks went too fast and they reluctantly boarded the plane to New York. Petuccini wasn't sure what they were returning to. *I wonder how the senator's research is going* was the last thought in his mind before he dozed off, leaning back in his comfortable first class seat.

~

Senator Hopkins was wondering the same. He had been getting daily reports from Zack on his so far fruitless research into Brady's activities. Boring, endless meetings; drives across the country in a campaign bus; eventless flights surrounded by journalists; exactly what you would expect from a political campaign. Nothing to confirm his suspicions, nothing he could use against Brady.

Finally, he instructed Zack to concentrate on Brady's home and film any meetings with visitors. The theory was that Brady would want maximum privacy if he had anything, or anyone, to hide. A couple of days later an excited call came from Zack: "Senator, I think you should come over. You want to see this as soon as possible."

When he arrived, Zack had a dazed look on his face.

"Do you want to see the film clip I took, or watch it in real time? I first saw it this morning, when I was tracking his movements on last Wednesday.

"Show me in real time, Zack." Hopkins nodded, his throat constricted with anticipation.

The 'Time Scope' was already tuned to the right coordinates. When it focused, they saw Brady talking to another man, stepping in menacingly close and gesturing angrily. When at last he turned away, Hopkins recognized the pale, stricken face of Trevor Smythe, Brady's campaign manager. After a few moments' hesitation, the young man quietly left the house. Brady walked briskly to the back hall, where he unlocked a heavy door. The Tracker followed him into a room furnished as a military operations centre. Zack fiddled with the knobs and panned across the entire room, finally coming to rest on the longest wall, entirely covered by a map of the world, showing different icons pinned on various countries.

Some of these icons were American flags, some were tanks, fighter planes and ships. Two were mushroom shaped clouds. They could see clearly: one over North Korea, one over Iran.

Zack adjusted the controls to scan the adjacent shorter wall, that displayed a gallery of portraits, all framed and hung in a neat row. Zack zoomed in on the images one by one: Julius Cesar,

Alexander the Great, Napoleon, Rommel, Goering, Hitler, Stalin, Patton, Sherman and MacArthur. At the end was a self-portrait in full military regalia.

The camera moved back to Brady, who walked to a closet and opened the door to display sets of different military costumes, hanging limp, waiting to be favourite of the day. They watched in shocked silence as Brady pulled out a jacket and donned it over his shirt and slacks. It looked very much like the Wehrmacht uniform of Hermann Goering, complete with medals.

He walked up to Hitler's portrait, and saluted smartly. It was the Nazi salute. Zack focused on Brady's expression which frightened them both: his face was distorted in a hateful rage, devoid of sanity.

"You have the film of this?" Hopkins asked, once he was able to speak again.

Without a word, Zack handed over a small memory card.

"Thank you Zack," Hopkins put his hand on the young man's shoulder. "You may have just saved our country, probably the whole world. All I need now is to decide how to use it to stop this madman."

"Good luck, sir, and I mean it!" Zack matched the senator's tone with a mature voice of his own. "I hope you succeed."

On the way home, Hopkins reflected that he would never forget this moment. The images were etched onto his retina and into his brain with frightening intensity. He was sorry that he would have to subject Muriel to the same shock.

Chapter 8

"What are you going to do?" Muriel asked after she saw the clip.

"I'm not sure. I must do something, but I have to think it through. I have only one shot at this, and if I blow it, tragedy is almost certain." Gordon replied.

"Maybe you should have a conference with everyone in the time scope project and hear all opinions and ideas."

"You mean Petuccini and Zack too?" Hopkins looked surprised. "You think?"

"They know about the device and about the danger," Muriel seemed more and more excited by the thought. "What can it hurt to hear their thoughts as well? You need all the help you can get."

"True, but I don't have much time. If I'm to stop Brady, it has to be soon, while there is some hope for sane minds to prevail. Okay, I'll send a message to Petuccini to get in touch with me ASAP. I'm told he's home and has had a few days to clear the vacation mist out of his head."

"Do that, Gordon," Muriel said softly, "and, if it's not too much trouble to host me and the dogs until this is resolved, I'd like to be included as well."

"I wouldn't dream of doing it without you."

They didn't need to say any more, They were a team again, just like old times. Common danger brought them closer together.

"I'm only sorry for the dogs," Muriel added. "I'll have to take them for long walks every day, maybe the new smells will cheer them up."

"I can help you with that," Gordon volunteered. "I need the exercise."

~

By mutual agreement, they met at Zack's house, partly because the 'Time Scope' was there and they might need it to make their plans, partly because Senator Hopkins still wanted to meet Petuccini in a neutral and private place.

The others were already in Zack's living room, sitting in their usual places, when Hopkins and Muriel arrived. They had seen the video and were past the shock. Not past enough to take the danger lightly.

"What do you all think I should do with this information?" Gordon opened the conference and looked around the table. "The objective is to make Brady withdraw from the race."

"Too bad he has so much security protecting him all the time, or I could take care of it," Petuccini muttered.

"So, how about if we email him the video clip and threaten to make it public, unless he stops?" asked Zack.

"He would just claim it was filmed in Hollywood by his liberal enemies," Gordon dismissed the idea, "and his supporters would believe it."

"What if we contacted Homeland Security, show them the video and explain how we obtained it?" Muriel asked. "Never mind," she amended, "this is a dumb idea. I shudder to think what they would use the 'Time Scope' for, after."

"They'd never let me keep it!" Zack was alarmed. "I need it for my private eye career!"

"Relax, Zack," Petuccini chuckled. "None of us wants the feds to get hold of it."

"The biggest problem I see," Gordon explained, "is authenticating the video, without revealing the source. We *must* have direct eyewitness observation of that room. Preferably by journalists, for maximum exposure."

"Suppose," Muriel rubbed her chin thoughtfully, "someone in his camp invited the press to Brady's home? Preferably when he's far away, on a campaign trip. Show them around, including the 'war room'? It should be someone we could convince to cooperate. Maybe by showing him or her the video and explaining the risk?"

"I know Trevor Smythe, his campaign manager," Gordon picked up the thought. "He's a decent guy. He can't possibly know Brady's true colours. Problem is, Brady keeps the room locked."

"That's no problem," Petuccini sounded confident. "Give me ten minutes and I will take care of that lock."

None of them being able to offer a better idea, they agreed to leave it with Hopkins and hope that he could recruit Trevor Smyth to their cause.

~

Trevor Smythe thought it only slightly odd to get an invitation from Hopkins. They belonged to the same party and had met occasionally, He thought the senator wanted to pump him for information about the status of the campaign. At *his home? Maybe he doesn't want to be overheard.*

His first surprise was Muriel. He knew of her and thought it was strange that Gordon's ex-wife would be present, but it would have been rude to comment. Anyway, estranged couples make up sometimes. Very soon that surprise was dwarfed by the real one they had in store.

"Trevor, I'd like to show you a short video. I ask you to look at it very carefully and think of all the implications before you react," Hopkins said and clicked the 'Play' button on his notebook. They watched the scene without speaking, and continued silent for minutes after. All the while, Trevor kept rubbing his forehead, unaware of doing it.

Finally, he found his voice and croaked out: "Where did you get this?"

"I can't tell you that, Trevor, but I assure you, it is authentic."

"How can I be sure?" Trevor was clutching at straws now. "Maybe somebody photo-shopped it, or whatever they do to create fake videos!"

The senator and his lady exchanged meaningful glances. She nodded encouragement, and he leaned forward to look hard into Trevor's eyes.

"Have you seen this room in his house before? Are you in his confidence?"

"No, I haven't. It's at end of the hall and I never had any reason to enter it." Trevor said defensively.

"If I can arrange for you to see inside, would that convince you?" Hopkins asked earnestly.

"How could you do that? If this video is authentic, Brady would never let me in."

"Doesn't he trust you?"

"Not with sensitive material. Actually, he doesn't think all that much of me.... "

"Then, we'd have to look when he's not at home," Hopkins said thoughtfully. "unfortunately, that's illegal - a serious crime. But consider the alternative."

"Assuming it's true, what would you want me to do?"

"We need you to call a press conference at Brady's house. When the journalists arrive, and the candidate doesn't, pretend that you'd mixed up the dates, apologize and then show them around, including that room."

"Basically, you're asking me to choose between my boss and a felony. Some choice!" Trevor summarized their situation. "But if this is true, a felony might be the lesser of two evils. Before I give you an answer, I must see the inside of that room with my own eyes. Arrange that, and "I'll consider your proposition."

"I understand," Gordon didn't argue. "When would it be possible?"

"He's flying to Seattle day after tomorrow, I'm to join him Friday," Trevor replied, after briefly looking at his cellphone to confirm Brady's schedule. "That works for you?"

"I'm sure we can make it work." Gordon stood up and looked Trevor in the eye. "Let me know what time and we'll meet you there."

"This was a major shock to me, senator," Trevor admitted, his voice not too steady. "I've been worried about the general for some time, but I never suspected anything this sinister. Don't think I'll sleep tonight."

"Join the club. We haven't slept much since we first saw that video." Gordon accompanied his guest to the door and clasped his hand in parting. "I'll be waiting for your call, Trevor."

"Good bye, Senator Hopkins. And God help us all!"

~

Trevor had the security code to Brady's house, as he had to fetch papers, a speech or a change of clothes for his candidate. The door to the back room, however, was always locked. Petuccini, true to his word, had it open in less than ten minutes. Skills acquired in his misspent youth were still at his fingertips.

The three men trooped in, turned on the light and stopped in the middle of the "war room" – there was no other way to refer to it, unless you wanted to call it a 'bunker'.

Trevor walked around slowly, examined everything carefully, without touching. He spent a long time in front of the map, studying Brady's plan for world conquest. With the end of his necktie on the handle, he briefly opened the closet to assure himself that the uniforms existed, then proceeded to the 'gallery', all the time shaking his head in disbelief.

"The son of a bitch really means it!" Petuccini exclaimed, as he viewed the display.

Hopkins just stood there, by the table in the middle of the room, finally realizing that the scene wasn't a nightmare to wake up from.

There was a computer on a desk and scattered papers with handwritten notes. "Maybe Zack could hack into his computer and see what other excrement he can dig up," Petuccini suggested, but Smythe shook his head. "No need for that, I've seen enough."

Hopkins touched his arm. "Trevor, I know it's a shock, a lot to take in. But time is short. Are you with us?"

"Let me talk to the general, just once," Trevor pleaded. "I've got to assure myself I've tried everything short of stabbing him in the back."

"I would call it saving your country from tragedy." Hopkins muttered.

"Maybe it's just a fantasy, a hobby. Maybe he doesn't mean any of it!" Trevor was almost in tears. "I must be *sure* I'm doing the right thing."

"All right, Trevor, but time, as I said, is *very* short. We're entering the final phase of the campaign. You know the election is in only four weeks."

"I'll talk to him in Seattle tomorrow." Trevor's voice had a tone of finality.

They left the room and Petuccini carefully relocked it.

"I'm awaiting your call, Trevor. I hope you'll be strong enough to do the right thing. And please make sure you don't let slip that you're aware of his little fantasy!"

"Don't worry about that. If he really means … all this…," Trevor said as they walked to their cars, "the bastard doesn't deserve my loyalty."

~

"You can be sure that I fucking mean it!" Brady's barked at Trevor, who had spent the last five minutes trying to convince his boss to moderate his rhetoric on foreign policy. "I thought you had more guts than that, Trevor. It's not too late to replace you with somebody who's got a backbone!"

"I'm not worried about what you'll do as president," Trevor lied. "I want to see to it that you get enough votes to *become* president!"

"Don't worry about the votes, you chickenshit. Just make sure you organize the last four weeks with your usual efficiency. *That's* what I recruited you for, not psycho-babble."

"Still, do you think citing the possibility of major military confrontation is going to win votes?"

"Have you heard the crowd respond? The whistles, the cheers, the clapping and stomping? My people are ready for bold action!"

"How about the general public? The millions who don't attend your rallies? You need their votes too!"

"And I'll get them, don't you worry!" Brady was shouting now. "It's time to be *decisive*. I wish those ninnies at the end of world war two had more guts. We could have kept on going and demolished the Russkies. We had the bomb then and they didn't.

Now it's too late, but we still can clobber the uppity kaffirs in Iran and North Korea!"

Trevor didn't need to hear more. He had his proof. After reassuring Brady that he would be his diligent and reliable soldier and returned to his own hotel room, he called Hopkins. All he said was: "I'm in."

~

The newspaper headlines three days later were in the largest font the papers could muster. "Presidential Nominee's Bunker"; "War Hero Closet Nazi!"; "Shocking Revelations about Front-runner!"; "General Plans Word War Three" and on and on and on.

The FBI announced an immediate investigation into Brady's foreign connections; Homeland Security denied any knowledge of Brady's secret Nazi leaning; Brady's party convened an emergency meeting. It was unthinkable to support their nominee after these revelations; he would have to withdraw. They had three weeks to replace him. There was no historical precedent.

Nobody worried about how the discovery had been made. Trevor Smythe's explanation of mixing up the dates was brushed aside as irrelevant. The photos of Brady's 'war room' and the viral video clip of Brady saluting Hitler's portrait, swept aside any argument. General

Brady disappeared from the public eye, presumably hiding from the army of reporters that all wanted a piece of him.

When Gordon Hopkins was summoned by the National Committee, he did not know what to expect. He could not imagine how they might have discovered his role in this mess, but he was still a little concerned. He was unprepared for what they had in store for him.

"Gordon, sorry for the urgency," Mike Sutherland, the party chairman, greeted him. "But we are desperate. We have three weeks till the election and we need a new candidate. We can't start a new process at this point, have to go with the most popular ranking party member. We overwhelmingly voted for you. Do you accept?"

Gordon needed to sit down. This was something he had never aspired to; never dreamed of. All he wanted was to retire and leave this constant drama behind. Suddenly, in his mind, he saw the Vermont forest with the log house, Muriel at her carving bench, happy dogs chasing each other outside on the leaf-covered lawn, and knew, beyond shadow of a doubt that he did *not* want to be president.

~

The three conspirators met for the last time in Zack's living room. They had a decision to make regarding the 'Time Scope'. Zack owned it, but they all felt it was their common responsibility.

"So, kid, what do you intend doing with it?" Petuccini asked. There was more respect in his voice than he had ever shown that young man.

"You know my plans," Zack replied. "I'll start searching for my first...ahem.. second client tomorrow morning."

"It's not that simple, Zack," Gordon explained gently. "This is a very dangerous device in the wrong hands and, now that we are aware of it, we want to make sure that it's used only for legitimate purposes."

"You can trust me on that by now." Zack objected, but Petuccini interrupted him.

"I have thought of a possible solution, if both of you agree." He turned from one to the other. "What if I hire you, Mister Dougall, as a technical expert in my casino, with salary and flexible hours, to supervise our security system maintenance and upgrade?"

"You're kidding!" they both exclaimed, but Petuccini wasn't deterred. "Most of the time you would pursue your own business activities, but I could keep an eye on you and on what you do with the gadget."

Zack was speechless, but Hopkins was not. "I have a counter suggestion. What if we set up a company for Zack, invest in it financially, so that he can get a decent office and all the equipment he needs? Then we *both*," he looked pointedly at Petuccini, "can keep an eye on him, his device and his activities? Would that suit you, Zack?" He turned to the kid, who kept swiveling his head from one of his 'mentors' to the other.

"That would be a lot better for me," he enthused. "I have no intention of moving to Ocean City or getting involved with a casino. If you help me start up, I'll give you unlimited access to the Scope and all three of us can make sure that it's used properly."

"Well, that's a thought... and a disappointment," Petuccini admitted. "But there is some logic and justice in this plan. Count me in."

"That's great, Zack, because I would like to do some research for a book and I need to check historical facts." Hopkins laid out his own agenda.

With all three in agreement, the rest of the meeting was devoted to discussing the new premises Zack would need.

Zack Dougall was on his way to open a detective agency, Joe Petuccini was on his way back to his Casino and his Maria. Gordon Hopkins was on his way to a serious discussion with Muriel, concerning his decision to retire from politics and maybe spend a lot more time in Vermont, if she was agreeable to the idea.

Chapter 9

I know Maria has been keeping things together, Peticcini reflected on the plane, *very competently. However, it just might be time to take a close look at my business and decide what I want to do in the long run.*

As expected, she was waiting at the airport and it was obvious from the way she greeted him, that she had missed him too.

"Well, how did it go?" she asked. Petuccini was uncertain how much to tell her. He had promised not to divulge the existence of the device to no-one. But he hated to keep secrets from Maria. Besides Hopkins had told *his* wife. In business, a person cannot trust very many people. Having broken with his family, Maria was Joe's only confidant.

Maybe it's time to think about starting a family of my own, maybe it's not too late? I wonder how she would feel about that?

This thought kept persisting in the back of his mind, during the drive home, during their happy reunion in the bedroom, during the evening news that they watched in bed.

We can't be more domestic than this. Why should we not make it permanent? What if I ask her right now?

The news was wall to wall coverage of the Brady scandal and Maria was mystified by how that YouTube video could have been acquired. "Someone must have bugged his room with hidden cameras," she speculated. "Who could have had access?"

"Good question." Joe managed to say, feeling slightly guilty.

"I mean," she persisted, "how could they come and go undetected? And there had to be two or three cameras if you look at the angles!"

"It's a mystery, for sure." Petuccini was unable to find a more appropriate comment without straight out lying.

"You don't seem to have much to say," she prompted. "Have you thought about this at all?"

"I have had other things on my mind, honey. We might as well discuss them now." Petuccini decided to dive in at the deep end. "We have known each other for two years now and have been very close for most of that time. How do you feel about escalating things?"

Maria was speechless.

"I mean to make our relationship permanent. If you think you might like to team up with an old scoundrel like myself?"

"Joe, what are you talking about? Are you teasing me?"

"Maria, I am an old fashioned Italian. I do not joke about family issues. I am asking you if you would consider marrying me and starting a family!"

There was a long silence from the other side of the bed.

"Did you hear what I asked?" Petuccini was nervous now. He knew if she said no, that would be the end of their relationship. He could not live with rejection, not at his age and position.

"I did, Joe, and I'm still in shock. Give me a minute to pull myself together. I don't think I ever told you that I love you, but I do. I never thought that you might feel the same way, so it's completely new to me. If you're really serious, then yes. I would be very happy to marry you and start a family."

Now it was Joe's turn to be speechless. This is what he had hoped for and dared not expect.

"Joe, tell me now if you weren't serious!" Maria almost shouted the question. "If you weren't, we can pretend that this conversation never happened and go back the way we were, but I need to know your answer NOW!"

Joe finally found his voice.

"I was serious, Maria and, unbelievable as it is, we seem to have just agreed to get married."

The rest of the evening and most of the night was spent on planning their life together. Nothing else was said about the Brady scandal that night.

~

There must have been something in the air that night because Gordon and Muriel were also having a heart to heart discussion in his home, as they watched the evening news together.

The big drama was over, they had won and a major disaster had been averted. The country was in the grip of anxiety over the upcoming election, with the conclusion almost certain. One party being without a credible candidate, the opposition's victory was guaranteed. Still, endless discussions and merciless soul-searching occupied the pundits. Questions of why no-one had suspected for so long, and how the truth finally came to light would keep journalists busy for months to come.

Gordon and Muriel knew that their role was over and were the happier for it. They didn't need this level of excitement and were ready to put it all behind them.

"Have I mentioned the caucus asked me to accept nomination for president?" Gordon had reluctantly decided to tell her, embarrassing though it was.

"No, you have not. Obviously, it slipped your mind! Such an insignificant tiny item of news can easily fall out of your head, at your age." Her eyes twinkled saying this and it took Gordon a second to catch on. "And did you?" she continued in the same semi-serious tone "Have you written your acceptance speech yet?"

"Take it easy, Muriel! You know damn well they asked out of desperation. That ticket could only ever have been a lead balloon, and they knew it."

"Weren't you even tempted? It would have been a feather in your cap anyway, win or lose, and the exposure would have greatly enhanced your career!" Muriel was now completely serious, offering Gordon an opportunity to talk about his future plans.

He did not waste it. "This career is over. I've made up my mind to retire from politics. I've had a long run, had some fun, won a few victories, made things a little easier for a few people. It's time to close the account."

Muriel raised an eyebrow. "And what are you going to do with yourself in retirement? I can't see you in a rocking chair, twiddling your thumbs for the next twenty years."

"You're right about that." Gordon plunged ahead, hoping for a sympathetic and supportive response. "I'm going to begin serious research into the history and meaning of the US Constitution for a book. It's time people understood the foundation of our country and our government."

"Why, that's great! Gordon, I can't imagine anything you'd be better suited for!" As an afterthought, she added. "Could you use Zack's gadget for that research?"

"As a matter of fact, I'm planning to do exactly that. And, incidentally, make sure the kid stays on the straight and narrow."

"So, are you ready to dive in and transform your house into a writer's lair? You should have a roll-top desk, I always admired those."

"Actually, I was thinking a vacation before my term ends, somewhere quiet, to think things through in peace. My life has been somewhat hectic of late," Gordon said ruefully.

"I have an idea, for you to consider," Muriel's voice was hesitant and cautious. "Why don't you come up to Vermont and spend a couple of weeks?

Plenty of quiet in the woods, and the dogs hardly ever bark."

"Do you mean it, Muriel? Don't you think it might lead to complications?"

"The only complications I can imagine are those that we consent to. We're adults; we know each other well enough. I will trust you if you do the same."

There was nothing more to say. They both knew where they had come from, where they were in their lives and where they might end up again - if things worked out as they hoped.

~

Zack and Suzy had an argument. Zack told her about Petuccini's offer of a job and how he had refused.

"Are you out of your mind?" Suzy couldn't keep her voice down. "This sounds like a once in a lifetime opportunity and you *refused*? I can't believe it!"

Zack looked at his girlfriend with calm, steady eyes, something Susan wasn't used to. He somehow seemed to have grown up during the last month. He acted with a quiet confidence that was new to her. New, and very attractive.

"So, it looks like we'll discuss it now," he said. "I know that you always wanted me to have a steady job, but that wouldn't be me. I like my freedom too much. I *don't* want to be under anyone's thumb. An independent businessman is what I want to be, and now I have the opportunity. This is who I am. You might as well accept it because I won't change."

Suzy wanted to interrupt, but Zack wasn't finished. "Besides, you *liked* the idea of starting a detective agency. With the help of the Scope, that's what I'm going to do".

"Well, I guess, if that's what you want, I can't stop you. But how will it affect us? I can't change who I am, either. I need stability and commitment in my life. Now I don't have either!"

"I have thought of that," Zack said calmly, "and I have a proposition to make."

"A proposition, or a proposal?" Susan could not keep sarcasm out of her voice.

"A little bit of both," Zack continued undeterred. "What I would like to do is start searching for my next client, and I could use your help."

"My help?" Susan was surprised. "How?"

"I can't entirely rely on the Scope. There's an awful lot of legwork to do, and I think you'd be good at interviewing people – you know, like witnesses and suspects. With your mind and body you can charm anyone into revealing information they'd never give me."

"Oh, sure, you think that flattery will melt me into a puddle?!"

"Seriously, Suzy, I would like you to consider moving in with me and quitting your job. With financial assistance from Hopkins and Petuccini, plus what I have left from my inheritance, we could live modestly for a year or longer even if no other money comes in."

"Seriously." She echoed. "You want me to move in. Aren't you afraid that I might never move out when you change your mind?"

She was still not quite sure how far she could trust him. This calm and confident Zack was new to her; maybe temporary.

"You should know I'm crazy about you. I've never looked at another girl since I met you. Next to the 'Time Scope', even way more than that, you're the most important thing in my life."

Susan was floored. She had not suspected this intensity of feeling from Zack; she had always thought that their relationship was a casual one, not for keeps: he was too immature.

"I need time to think about it, Zack." She gave him a brief hug, as if to reassure themselves that they were still the same two people. "In the meantime, how about going to Google to start searching for rewards? If I see that his madcap idea has a future to base a life and a relationship on, I will consider it. Seriously"

"That's fair," Zack conceded. "But do we have to do it right away?" he asked with an attempt at a straight face. "We haven't had our aerobic exercise for a few days and I may be losing my touch".

Susan rolled her eyes.

"Oh you men never change, it's always pleasure before work with you."

"Let's find out how we can combine the two." Zack laughed and went to his bar to pour drinks and turn on the stereo.

Search for Intelligence

by Francis Mont

The old man lived alone. He hadn't had a human companion for a long time - his children grown and gone, his wife bailed out years ago. He seldom talked to human beings, his once a week trip to Loblaws for food and sundries was the only contact he had with bipeds.

He wasn't lonely though, he had animated conversations with himself, mostly about aliens. He knew that they were out there and was determined to find them. His house was full of computer equipment, and the little money he could save from his pension was all eaten up by his several broadband internet accounts - his lifeline to the outside world. More precisely, to the off-planet world.

He was a passionate SETI-at-home member, downloading data twenty four hours a day, onto his eight high speed computers, processing the packets he was given from the big Arecibo radio telescope that had been searching the sky for signs of extra-terrestrial intelligence.

In 1999 SETI-at-home was started, distributing the collected data to millions of voluntary home computer users, so their number-crunching power could be added to the supercomputer's at Berkley. When he discovered SETI, the old man changed. He spent all their savings on computers, internet connection, network equipment. He locked himself into his basement workshop for most of the day, stopped talking to his wife of 47 years, coming up only for infrequent meals.

When every effort Sandra made to reach him had failed, she disappeared from the house one day, the old man hardly noticed. He kept going from one computer to the other, hoping for confirmation from Berkley that he had made contact.

There had to be intelligence somewhere in the universe, because he had given up, long ago, trying to find any on Earth. When his youngest son was blown up in Afghanistan, the old man was finished with the human race. He continued watching the news for a while still, and every day he was more and more convinced that his decision was justified.

He saw a species that was fast destroying the planet with its toxic waste, had thousands of nuclear warheads on hair trigger alert aimed at each other's cities, each other's wives and children, tolerated mass hunger and disease on large areas of the planet while their rich wallowed in ostentatious luxury. Their leaders were corrupt and power mad, they warped their citizens' minds with irrational religious dogma and racial hatred.

After a while he had had enough, stopped watching the news, stopped talking to his friends, stopped even thinking about humans. His eyes were glued to the dance of pulsating multicolour signals across the screens, waiting, waiting, waiting.

The postman who delivered the telegram from Berkley, found the front door open and, getting no answer to his knocks, walked in for the required signature.

He found the old man's body slumped forward in his chair, his hand still holding a pen over the last scrawled message on his notepad.

It said: "they are out there, intelligence must exist somewhere!"